Unlived
Affections

GEORGE SHANNON
Unlived
Affections

A CHARLOTTE ZOLOTOW BOOK

HARPER & ROW, PUBLISHERS, New York
Grand Rapids, Philadelphia, St. Louis, San Francisco,
London, Singapore, Sydney, Tokyo

Library of Congress Cataloging-in-Publication Data
Shannon, George.
    Unlived affections / George Shannon.
        p.   cm.
    "A Charlotte Zolotow book."
    Summary: At his grandmother's death, seventeen-year-old Willie
finds a box of old letters which explain many family secrets.
    ISBN 0-06-025304-5 : S   (U.S.).—ISBN 0-06-025305-3 (lib.
bdg.) : S   (U.S.)
    [1. Grandmothers—Fiction.   2. Homosexuality—Fiction.   3. Death—
Fiction.]   I. Title.
PZ7.S5288Un 1989   88-31470
[Fic]—dc19   CIP
                                                                AC

Typography by Elynn Cohen
1   2   3   4   5   6   7   8   9   10
First Edition

To David Holter

Henceforth letter-writing had to take the place of all the affection that could not be lived.

Thornton Wilder
The Bridge of San Luis Rey

Unlived
Affections

1

After nine hours of roofing in the Kansas sun, Willie stood numb as the shower's wet heat beat down on his back. He was glad that he had the next day off even if there wouldn't be time to rest. As the cramps in his shoulders began to fade, he stretched and decided he'd swim later on, once the pool was closed. He'd been swimming almost every night since Grom had died and left him to live in the house alone.

"Four more weeks," he told himself as he bent his head down to catch the shower's full force. "Four more weeks and I'd have left her."

It had made no difference to Willie where he went to college. He'd finally picked Nebraska. He was leaving, not going to something else. He just meant to leave his grandmother, Ottawa and everything else like his parents had left him. But Grom had stolen his chance to leave her, by dying.

She'd died the third of August, just before his eighteenth birthday, and left everything to him. After her second heart attack, the middle of June, confined her to bed, she tripled his college savings account without telling him. It was her second heart attack that changed everything. After that she even let her gray hair grow in and didn't care who saw it. But since her funeral Willie was discovering her gray hair was the smallest of the truths she'd long kept hidden.

Willie opened his eyes and watched the water stream down his sun-browned chest and long pale legs. Yes. He'd definitely swim later tonight. First he had to get Grom's things ready for the auction tomorrow.

"Her junk," he whispered, trying to make it sound as insignificant as possible. He didn't want anything that wasn't in his own room. The house was already sold. Everything else could be gone by supper tomorrow, and he'd be free.

He sighed as he thought of Grom's belongings scattered in the yard for everyone to see. Now they'd all know he'd lived in a museum. Thanks to her wrapping everything in covers of plastic or twill, her furniture looked new, but was so out-of-date it belonged like period pieces in a second-hand store. Willie couldn't remember anything really new except the bedside phone and remote-controlled television he gave her when the doctor ordered her to stay in bed. She insisted on keeping the house as ordered as her nurse's office at school—everything with one, and only one, place. If something wore out, she replaced it with a duplicate. At a quick glance, a photograph of Grom anywhere in the house—except Willie's room—looked the same no matter what year it was taken.

Turning again to take the water's full beating on the base of his neck, Willie thought ahead to tonight's swim. For years he'd gone alone late at night when his friends thought he was home with Grom and Grom thought he was out with friends. For every date he'd really had, he'd lied about five and gone swimming instead.

Being on the school swim team had made it easy to copy a set of keys to the pool at school. Summers it was even easier with the city park pool. He only had to wait till it closed at ten, then climb the fence, and the pool was his private world again. He loved the full spent feeling that followed as much as he did the swimming itself; everything erased but his body and the rhythm of breathing and strokes. It was the one place he felt in charge and alive.

Willie turned his face into the center of the shower's spray and felt himself swimming lap after lap. Lap after lap away from—

"Damn it!" he yelled, grabbing at the faucets to

stop the icy water that had slapped him back to the foggy bathroom. "Why didn't you yell at me to turn it off like you always do?

". . . Did." he whispered.

Stepping out of the shower, he realized he'd left the last clean towel by his bed that morning. No trouble. He gave his head and arms a shake, then headed down the hall, pleased with his build and nakedness. Years of swimming and two summers working roofs had given his body a solid shape and easy gait. Willie grinned as he stepped in front of the window fan to dry. Grom would have had a fit even thinking that he'd do such a thing.

From the time he'd finished grade school and grown taller than Grom, she'd fussed to keep him covered up. He was proud of being one of the first his age to shave, but was only able to show it off once by letting his beard grow out. That time brought a long lecture from Grom on how she'd raised him to be a decent boy and not some bum. Willie remembered it clearly. It was one of the few times she'd looked directly into his eyes. And all the time she'd talked, her eyes had kept shrinking till they were sharp as snake-eye dice. She'd barely spoken to him for a week after that.

Feeling as dry as he could get on a humid August night, he pulled on a pair of old gym shorts and headed downstairs to eat whatever hadn't gone bad.

The cold pizza passed. Willie dropped into his TV chair, identical to Grom's, and quickly ate both pieces.

"Come on," he told himself. "Just dump the stuff in boxes and get it gone." But he didn't move.

From the week of Grom's first heart attack, in May, to this sticky night, the summer's heat had made everything feel like twice its weight and kept him coated with a film of sweat.

Willie gulped down some Coke and stared at the cracks in the walls that ran like veins beneath old paper skin. With the furniture moved around for the sale, the house had changed completely. Walls showed layers of dirt despite Grom's constant cleaning, and there was a pale square shadow everywhere there'd been a picture. With its order destroyed, the house looked as frail as Grom had just before she'd died.

Once he got everything in the yard ready for auction, he told himself, it wouldn't be Grom's house anymore. Her house was *full*. She'd kept every closet crowded, and the extra bedroom upstairs was never used for anything but boxes of her past. Old clothes sorted by color. Cards by season. Even all her magazines were boxed in monthly order back to October of 1967.

She'd kept their life as ordered as her past. Cleaning, weeding, washing and baking—each had its assigned day. Up at six thirty no matter what. Supper at five. Dishes at six. To bedrooms by ten. Wednesday had been her bridge club night, the only night she didn't watch TV, crochet and smoke.

Upstairs in bed Willie usually heard only bits of her TV shows, but on Wednesdays he'd hear Grom's other voice. Wednesday nights she laughed. Really laughed. It was the one night he stayed home no matter what.

The six other nights Grom crocheted. She couldn't watch TV without smoking, or smoke without her hands twitching hooks and thread into endless flowers. She'd kept her cigarettes in a crocheted holder, along with her hooks and thread, in an old cigar box that never left the side of her TV chair. Willie couldn't think of one of the objects without all the others, too. No one Grom had liked ever wanted for a bedspread, chair arm covers or a coaster set until this summer. One night in early June she'd suddenly put down her hooks and said, "Turn that thing off. My hands are too tired." That night Willie had swum laps until the sun began to rise.

"Come *on*," he said to himself, leaning back in the chair. "As soon as all this stuff is gone, *I'm* gone." Then he grabbed the doilies from the arms of his chair, tossed them at a box and headed upstairs.

Just inside his room Willie stopped and carefully pulled a poster off the ceiling. The room was so squat he didn't have to stretch. It was his oldest poster, turned yellow with age, a picture of a large submarine. Posters were the only way Grom had allowed him to alter his room. The most recent two were of several women in wet swimsuits. Knowing Grom would have hated them made them twice as sexy. Still, he hadn't dared to get them till her second attack in June, when she was told to stay in bed.

No matter what the picture, posters had always been a welcome escape from the wallpaper trains beneath them. As a child he'd picked the trains, pretending they could take him anywhere he wanted to go. But instead they'd taken him back again and again to the day he'd picked them out. It was the day he'd overheard Grom talking to his new second-grade teacher.

"It's the saddest story you'll ever hear," Grom was telling her when Willie came in early from lunch recess. "His father ran off and died before he was born; then my daughter and the fool she was dating were killed when a truck crashed into their car. I'm all he's got in the world."

When Grom and his teacher turned and saw Willie behind them, none of them was able to speak.

That afternoon Grom took him to pick out the wallpaper. All the way to the store and back, she talked about how a big boy like him should be picking out his own. That only hurt him more. He knew he was getting wallpaper because he'd heard the truth. That he'd found out her lie. She'd always told him that his mother had died from a bad heart the same as his grandpa had when his mother was a little girl.

For years he had rocked in his chair at night with his eyes shut tight trying his best to forget the trains as they circled his room in a closing coil.

Time and the posters had distanced those days and nightmares, but as Willie continued pulling his posters down, the trains showed again, bringing that day back to life. For a moment he thought of gouging out chunks of the wallpaper trains, then instead began to slowly tear up the posters, beginning with the one of the submarine. To see the trains again made him angry at not having been told the truth *and* angry at having to know it.

Willie stuffed the torn posters in the trash. He'd already decided to leave everything behind except his records, stereo, two boxes of clothes and his old rocking chair. If forced to choose, he'd have left his stereo before he'd have left the chair. When Grom had tried to throw it out once when he was small, he'd screamed, "Don't touch it! It's mine. Mine to keep."

The chair was the one thing he had that he was certain he and his mother had shared. He remembered being rocked by his mother, but his proof was a photograph showing his mother and him sitting in it. His own plump face was laughing directly into the camera at Grom, who'd taken the picture. His mother's face was a smooth echo of Grom's, and all her attention glowed on him. He'd never seen anyone else with such long cascades of curly hair. Willie looked at the picture so often it was wrinkled and smudged. It was always a comfort; always there waiting for him.

It was almost all he knew of his mother as a mother. Grom was full of stories about her daughter, but only as a little girl.

"But I mean what was she like when she was my *mom?*" he'd ask at the end of one of Grom's stories. But the only answer he got would be another story of Grom's dear little girl. To hear Grom, his mother had been perfect at everything in school. And "She always had the prettiest hair. I brushed it two hundred times every night."

Questions about his father brought trouble. Especially asking what he looked like. Grom acted as if he were begging for fancy toys.

"Gettin' only makes you want," she'd scold. "You're better off without."

Afraid of her anger, he usually let it pass, but once in the fourth grade he'd been determined to get an answer.

"But I just want to know if he looked like me."
"No."
"What did he do?"
"No."

"What was he like?"

"No."

"Why did he run away? Didn't he want me?"

"No," Grom had snapped. "No. You're better off without him. He's unfit to be a father and he's better off dead."

Though the questions remained as strong as ever in his thoughts, Willie never asked Grom after that. It wasn't so much her sharp words that made him stop, or the lack of answers, but the silence that followed. For hours afterward Grom would ignore him, making him feel erased. Then she'd call him to supper and act like nothing had happened.

Silence had been the hardest and surest thing about living with Grom. Willie always looked forward to the calming quiet he felt when he swam alone. But Grom's silence was like the heavy, nervous quiet of listening for the gun at the start of a race. And when he wasn't waiting for the silence to end, he was waiting for its painful return.

Willie looked around his bedroom. "Done."

Everything was packed or in the trash except the dresser and bed, and they'd be sold at the auction. He'd be gone and in his dorm in Nebraska within the week.

Carefully, he carried the rocker downstairs, going slowly so he wouldn't nick the wood. His mother's or not, he would have liked it. It was the only piece of furniture in the house that didn't have a thousand look-alikes.

He set it down in the living room by his packed-up stereo and turned on the TV. Then, without even watching to see what was on, he went into Grom's bedroom, turned on her set, and went outside to water the flowers.

Grom's flowers had been off limits, which had been fine with Willie. But this summer, confined to bed, she'd had to let him care for them. He'd missed her working in the garden as much as she had. In the yard she grew softer, humming as she worked to keep each flower bed a patch of pure color, free of weeds. From Willie's window upstairs the yard looked like a giant paint box.

As soon as the sky began to dim, she'd nag Willie to water the flowers and pick the dead blooms. He grumbled as much as she nagged, but the nightly ritual gave them their most comfortable times together. Flowers and seeds could be discussed with ready answers, unlike her heart and Willie's leaving for college. Neither could bear to talk those truths.

As long as she heard the water running Grom would quietly rest, but once it was off she began calling through her window again.

"Are the poppies still blooming?"

"Handfuls." he answered, though the last had bloomed in June.

13

"And the geraniums?"

"Enough for three baskets."

"And have you checked the ones on your mother's stone?"

"They're fine."

"And my glads. Are they out? They're my favorite, you know."

"Soon, I'm sure. Before you know it."

Flower by flower Willie would call out the evening's inventory as he knew she dreamed it to be, often surprising himself by the number of flowers he'd learned to name.

"I just wish I could see them." she said each night as he finished. "This is the best garden in years."

Willie, the doctor and the visiting nurse had all told her she could take a wheelchair ride to the garden. But fears of another attack and the wish to keep the garden as Willie described it kept her in bed. She knew from Willie's answers he was lying about the flowers, but she liked it. She was happy to imagine the garden he was creating and even happier that he was creating it for her.

"Would you like a bouquet?" Willie would ask on cue.

"No. No," she'd say. "I'd rather think them alive outdoors than see them wilt inside. But take some more to Libby. She's such a sweet girl."

"If you want," he'd say, and caress her hand. And, for a while, he took some to Libby every night.

He'd liked Libby's laugh and mane of curly hair from the first day she'd transferred to school and into his senior English class. Still, he hadn't meant for their prom date to be anything more than one date. He planned to skip the prom altogether, but when she asked him, he said yes to get the swim team off his back.

They watched the crowning of the King and Queen, danced several dances and went through the buffet twice before the prom's first hour passed. They were sitting not knowing what to say next when Libby excused herself. Before long Willie heard giggles and looked up to see her coming back with a strip of toilet paper stuck to the heel of her bright-pink shoe. At first he wanted to hide, then run up and punch everyone who was laughing. But Libby was soon laughing too. She laughed louder than anyone else, ran to the rest room and came back out draped in a toilet-paper stole.

He'd never seen anyone so brave. Willie jumped up, grabbed her and began to dance. They danced and laughed as the streams of paper fell loose around the room. Then they danced out the door, laughing so hard that they were both holding their stomachs by the time they reached his car. Willie felt as spent and elated as if he'd just swum laps. And proud of Libby.

After that they saw each other every night and twice had supper with Grom. It was days before

Willie considered swimming at night. When he finally went, he took her along and their laughter echoed over the water.

He simply could not stop thinking about her. And when he was with her, he forgot about everything else. They talked for hours at a time. Willie knew that when he talked to her, Libby was really listening with her ears *and* eyes. One night after she told him of moving thirteen times with her salesman-father, Willie told her the few things Grom had told him about his invisible father and that he'd dreamed that his father was traveling like hers. He even told her how Grom had locked his mother's bedroom. It was the first time he'd told anyone. Unlike Grom, Libby would answer any question and, just as likely, ask any, too. After Grom's years of silence Willie found that exciting even when it startled him.

What had startled him most was how she brought up sex. One night at the pool they'd been talking about the flirty games some kids played just to be sure they had a date.

"Who needs it?" said Willie.

"Not me," she said with a smile as she slipped her hand inside his suit. "And not you."

Remembering, he felt like one big smile.

It was the first time they slept together.

But that was *then*, he told himself as he turned the hose on the bed of red dahlias. Besides, sex alone was easier. No expectations or babies to worry about. Alone it was always there when he needed it to make himself feel alive and in control.

The night the doctor told Willie that Grom had had a mild third attack and would likely die before autumn, Willie broke off with Libby. He just called, told her about Grom, said that he couldn't see her anymore, then hung up before she could talk. When the phone rang right away, Willie knew it was Libby calling back and left the room.

He was so frightened of being left that he truly believed if he left Libby, she couldn't leave him. She meant too much to him. That's what he'd meant to do with Grom and college. It made sense, he told himself. He wouldn't hurt as much if *he* left her. But he did.

The next night Libby was waiting when he got to the city park pool.

"Are you okay?"

"Yes."

"What's wrong?"

Willie had no words. He just wanted to leave.

"Is it your grandmother?"

He looked away.

"Talk to me. Please," said Libby, beginning to cry. "Let me listen."

God, how Willie wanted to talk, but words would only make him feel close to her again. He wanted to hold her and be held. But the fear of her leaving him, the way Grom was leaving him, was too great.

"I'm sorry," he said as he hurried away. "I'm sorry. I'm sorry."

Libby was the first girl he'd dated whom Grom had grown to like. The weaker Grom had gotten, the more she talked of how nice Libby was and how good it felt to know they had each other. All her talk was his excuse for never telling her they weren't a couple anymore.

One night when Willie told Grom he was bowling with friends, she called Libby over and gave her her favorite flower vase.

"It was my grandmother's," she told Libby. "My mother wanted me to give it back after I eloped with Willie's grandfather. We were as crazy for each other as you and Willie are."

Talking of Willie and Libby's being together, Grom looked more relaxed and relieved than she had all summer. Her face alone told Libby that Willie hadn't told her he'd broken it off.

Libby wasn't about to hurt her. She talked as if nothing had changed, kept smiling and promised to return to get flowers for the vase.

Willie was about to turn into the driveway when he saw Libby through the window. He drove on by. He knew Libby wouldn't break Grom's dream of them together. In the same breath he wanted to run thank her *and* hide so he wouldn't have to tell her good-bye again.

Now Willie took a deep breath and tried to concentrate on the garden. He loved the smell of fresh, water-soaked earth. He'd resented having to do all the watering in June and July, but now he did it lovingly. He wanted the new owners to see that Grom had kept the best garden in town. Watering also let him feel nothing had changed.

Tonight when he finished the flowers, he turned the water on himself.

"Wheewwwww!" he gasped with a welcome shudder. Lazily moving the hose over his shoulders and head, he gulped a drink as he arched his back, then stuck his thumb over the nozzle and laughed as he sprayed himself from head to toe. Quick as the shudder, he saw himself years before running around in his underpants, squealing, as Grom sprayed him while she watered the flowers.

"Damn," he said as he turned off the water. "Just pack the boxes and leave it be.

"Enough," he told himself, then shook his wet head and walked toward the house.

Back inside he flicked on the light in the kitchen, then went to Grom's room and flopped down on her bed. He still had to empty her closet. It was sure to be the most crowded of all. He reached for her phone and called Paul.

"Can you come over at six in the morning instead of seven?"

"Sure."

"I'll buy you breakfast. See you then."

As back-alley neighbors Paul and Willie had been best friends in grade school, but drifted further apart as each year passed. Paul loved football as much as Willie did swimming. And while Paul liked to be in the middle of things, Willie felt best staying far to the edge. It had only been this summer when they got jobs with the same construction firm that they'd talked again. Paul was the one person Willie felt able to ask for help moving the furniture. It seemed like just another part of their work.

Willie still had his hand on the phone when its ring made him jump. It was Libby.

"How're you doing? It took forever to sort my granddad's stuff when he died last year."

She sounded so sure and warm. He missed her. Even though he'd broken off two weeks earlier, he'd called her first the morning Grom died, just to hear her voice. Since then she called him every night. Sometimes he talked, sometimes he didn't. Nights he talked, he regretted it afterward. Talking meant more of a bond than he wanted. For Libby those same nights seemed a step toward the growing bond she wanted and felt.

"*Nobody* could beat my grandmother," he told her. "She saved enough crap to fill a department store. You should see . . ."

Willie fell silent. He'd done it again. What are

you telling *her* for? he scolded himself. Now she'll want to come over.

"You okay? How about if I come over for a bit?"

"No. NO." He was afraid to see her. "There's too much to do."

"You know you don't have to prove anything by doing it all alone," she told him. "I could—"

"I'm not!" snapped Willie. "I don't know why everybody thinks I should be so upset."

"Okay," said Libby softly. "Okay. I only meant I'd be glad to help. I just thought you might like some help. I'll see you at the sale. 'Bye. I miss you."

Willie stared at the phone as he slowly put down the receiver. He felt as heavy and stuck as the August air.

"Gone!" he told himself as he leaned back across Grom's bed. He'd leave the house and Libby both, locking the door behind him as tightly as Grom had locked the door to his mother's bedroom.

Deciding Grom's closet could wait a few minutes more, Willie stretched down into Grom's bed. Eyes closed, he slid his hand across his stomach, then down to his shorts as he slowly began to stroke himself. He was beginning to slide off his shorts when the phone rang again.

It was the woman next door asking him to hide the buffet till she could get to the sale.

"I'll try," he promised.

"I just can't think of her without thinking of that buffet. She always looked so happy sitting in front of it while we were playing cards."

"I'll try," he said again, wishing it were already sold. " 'Bye."

Willie sat watching Grom's little TV without really seeing what show was on till he suddenly noticed the room was black and the children playing tag next door had gone inside to bed.

It would be so easy, thought Willie, to just fall asleep and let people take whatever they wanted.

"Let *them* sort and move all the crap," he said as he stood up and turned on the light. But even as he fussed, he reached for Grom's old picture of Jesus in the garden and carefully placed it in the top of a box.

"Come *on*, Ramsey," he yelled with a clap of his hands as if coaching himself toward the end of a race. "Get your butt in the water and start makin' waves!"

2

By midnight Willie was glazed with sweat and felt
he'd never done a thing but carry boxes down the
narrow stairs. Grom had packed rows and stacks of
boxes in the extra bedroom, all labeled as neatly as
her medicines.

"Nothing but junk," muttered Willie as he grabbed
each box. "Junk."

Halfway through the boxes he dropped one by
accident and watched it stutter down the steps. After
that he gladly dropped the rest. It felt good to see
them land with a thud, especially when they split a
seam. Box after box got a bigger heave. Then, suddenly, he turned the last one upside down and
slammed it open on the railing's edge.

"Damn you!" he yelled as it dumped out a stream
of small photographs.

Exhausted, he let the box drop, then walked down the steps to the scattered pictures. Perhaps she'd kept a picture of his father after all. Quickly but thoroughly Willie raked his hands through the photographs. They were only the faces of grade-school kids.

"Damn you," he said again as he read the box's label: GRATEFUL PATIENTS. "Pictures of every friggin' kid who ever skinned a knee at school, but no pictures of my father. Nothing."

Willie kicked them aside and went to the kitchen. After checking all the cupboards and slamming them shut, he grabbed the bag of potato chips and went to Grom's room. Her TV was playing nothing but snow, but he didn't care. He just sat on the edge of her bed thinking of the work he still had to do. The only task left that wouldn't need Paul's help was emptying his mother's bedroom. He couldn't put it off anymore.

"No sweat," he slowly told himself as he ate the last chip. "Junk's junk." But as he walked up the stairs, his feet slowed down with every step.

Both his mother and her room had vanished overnight. One morning when he was two, Willie went to wake her up like he always did, but found her door locked. He was calling, "Wake up! Wake up!" when Grom ran up the stairs.

"Momma, wake up."

Grom scooped him up and hurried downstairs

shaking her head. She carried him for hours without saying a word, until a neighbor finally took him to get some ice cream.

After that day his mother's bedroom was always locked. He was told his mother had died, but as young as he was, it made no sense. He stopped asking when his mother was coming back because each time it made Grom cry.

It wasn't till he was in the fourth grade that Willie even learned that Grom had a key to his mother's room. One Saturday a month, when she thought he was busy playing, Grom would open the room and clean for an hour, then lock it up again. From the way she sneaked around those days, Willie knew it was her secret. She never did know that Willie knew about her visits.

When he finally learned to pick the lock a year later and got inside, Willie slowly and quietly cried. The room smelled old and stale, but as he sat on the bed, forgotten odors filled his senses and gently wrapped around him. The room and smells felt so friendly, he kept expecting his mother to walk in with his next breath. Even her geranium was still blooming by the window. It was then that Willie understood the room was something special, like his photograph of his mother and himself in the rocking chair, and deserved to be hidden away.

He'd been locking the door behind him when Grom caught him. She glared past his face and demanded to know why he was trying to break into a room that wasn't his.

"But it's Mom's room," he answered. He didn't tell her he'd already been inside.

"It *was*," she interrupted. "But now it's mine and private just like the extra bedroom."

With that encounter his mother's room became a secret that Willie and Grom each kept to themselves rather than a memory shared. It was as if his mother's room became invisible—never acknowledged or mentioned in any way.

As he stood facing the door tonight with no one to tell him he couldn't go in, Willie noticed how the door that had always seemed so tightly locked hung loose and crooked in its old frame. The other rooms had offered Willie an aggressive joy of dismantling the past that Grom had collected like bits of string. His mother's room was different. Knowing it hadn't been lived in or changed in sixteen years made him feel like it was a tomb that shouldn't be touched.

"Go calm, but quick," Willie said to himself as he picked the lock. He would do it just as he'd done the other rooms. "Empty the closets and drawers into boxes, then toss them downstairs. Less than an hour."

But as he opened the door and looked inside, his plans faded away. Dead air as hot as the workday's roof came out in a wave over Willie, who stood as still as all he saw. The whole room looked as faded and as distant as his third-grade picture in the dining room. As dried and forgotten as the dead-dry geranium near the window. Nothing had been dusted nor a window opened since Grom's first heart attack in May.

He knew the room hadn't changed since his mother's death or even since he'd first picked the lock, yet it didn't match his memory. Since her death both Willie and Grom had gradually created the woman each wished she had been. Willie had invented complete memories of things they'd done together. Even souvenirs they'd found together and brought back to her room. He'd had to. Grom's constant hymns to her perfect little girl had ground away the few true memories of the grown-up mother he'd had when he was two.

Willie didn't have even imagined memories of his father. He had nothing to build them on. He had no idea of who his father was or what he looked like. Grom's only description was her bitter "unfit to be a father and he's better off dead."

To fill the void, Willie had made up story after story for himself of what his father had done after he'd gone away, and how he'd died.

Though the face he gave his father and the details of the stories often changed, the basic plot remained the same. His father had died a hero saving someone else.

At school Willie's stories grew more and more exotic as he began to tell them to quiet those kids who teased him for having no father. When they doubted him, he felt as if he'd lost his father again. When they believed him, he felt that it might be true and dreamed of running off to the same adventures and finding him. Willie loved seeing their envy instead of the pity that always came from adults. For a while he'd even come to believe the story of his father's fatal mission on a spying submarine.

But by the seventh grade the kids were no longer interested in fathers *or* adventure stories. Without an audience Willie's stories to himself grew darker and laced with events that might have deserved Grom's angry silence. Robbing a bank. Beating his mother. Killing someone. The things that made men guilty and that got them shut away on TV shows. It was then that he started shutting out the questions even to himself. He felt ashamed of what the truth might be behind Grom's words and silence.

As he looked around his mother's dust-covered room, Willie thought of all the nights he'd gotten up and come to sleep outside her door. Not once had Grom ever been mad when she'd found him there in the morning.

"Come on . . ." he said as he rubbed his palm along the door frame. "Junk is junk."

One by one he dumped the dresser drawers into

boxes, paying as little attention as he could to what they held. His mother might be long dead, but it was still her dresser. And besides, he knew that even though they were full of things his mother had liked years ago, they weren't her. Finding out what perfume she'd used and what clothes she'd worn didn't tell him what she'd felt, if she'd been happy or why his father had run away.

Clothes and shoes from the closet filled four more boxes. To Willie's surprise, his mother's room soon proved the easiest to clean out. Emptying the downstairs had gouged out hole after hole of where Grom wasn't anymore. But he'd missed this room for most of his life. By now it held no more life than the dead geranium.

Handful by handful Willie tucked his mother's postcards into the odd spaces left in boxes. She'd kept them stuck around her dresser's big mirror like a wreath. They were all addressed to her and almost all were from foreign countries. Half even had her old name—Kate Davenport—instead of Ramsey like his.

When he got to the magazines on the bedside table, he paused. All four were from the month of his mother's death.

Maybe Grom was right, Willie thought as he tossed them into the box of trash. The room *hadn't* had much to do with his mother since Grom had locked the door, keeping life out and the past inside.

"At least she had friends," he reasoned aloud as he went through her big flat-topped oak desk.

One drawer held more postcards addressed to her and others without any messages or stamps. Another drawer held nothing but an old cigar box like Grom's filled with stamps and envelopes, and a small address book.

"Maybe . . ."

As quickly as he could, Willie thumbed to the R's. No Ramseys. Then the D's. No Davenports either.

"Figures," he grumbled, and dropped it in the box of trash. "Me and me alone."

The big bottom desk drawer was filled with file folders of old class notes. Most were nothing but pages of numbers. Willie just shook his head and began throwing them out three and four at a time, but stopped when the last few folders fell over. There was a shoe box wedged in the back of the drawer.

"She was a regular post office!"

The box held a six-inch stack of letters bound with a rubber band so old it began to crumble at his touch. It made sense that they were all to his mother, but flipping through them Willie saw that the handwriting was the same on every one, as was the name in the return address.

Bill Ramsey. Bill. The name frightened and excited him.

"But why wasn't his name in the address book?"

Who cares? he told himself. He had the letters. Willie took the box and headed to the kitchen as calmly as he could. The name was too close to his own to let him think anything other than what he wanted most to believe. That he was finally holding something of his father's in his hand.

Here, suddenly, was hope of finding answers. Of finding out what Grom had always refused to tell. Willie carefully laid the box on the kitchen table, sat down, stood up, then sat down again. Hesitantly he took the top letter from the pile. The paper was so light, so frail to the touch, it seemed as if the mildest breeze could steal it away.

The Kentucky return address must mean they were love letters, he decided, from before his parents were married.

No good, he realized. They already have the same last name. But what were they doing in different states . . . the army?

Willie's hands moved quickly but gently as he opened the first yellowed envelope, then pulled its letter free. From the first words he read, everything else—the room, the heat, the work to be done—began to fade.

3

August 22, 1964

Dear Kate,

I'm here. Finally. It felt like twice as many days cramped up on the bus. And I know you can't be, but I wish you were here. I talked to you all through the trip, wishing I could show you things. My rooming house seems nice enough, though the bunch next door are playing their radio as if they're deaf and all twangy songs with people singing through their noses. Two days on the bus and I still can't fall asleep. Once I get things straight with Mr. Whitehead and find my way around town, maybe I can find a quieter and cheaper place to stay. Is it still burning up at home? It's warm and sticky here, but there's a nice breeze tonight. There are hills everywhere. When the bus pulled into town, it was like going into some faraway time. Back to other worlds and back to when I was a kid on family trips down here. I'd forgotten, if I ever knew, how funny Kentucky people talk. When I was dragging my boxes off the bus, this guy about our age said, "Hepya?" I said, "What?" He just yelled it again and then grabbed one of my boxes. I finally figured out he was saying "Help you?"

The first thing I unpacked was my chest of tools, but they suddenly seem so old and inferior. I know I want to be here, but right now I'm more lost than happy. Here to you feels a whole lot farther than there to here did before I left. And what if Whitehead thinks I'm a fool?

Well, the music next door has finally stopped, so maybe I can fall asleep. Smile at your mother for me. And lots of everything to you. It sure would be nice to wake up next to you in the morning. Take care and don't let your boss boss you around too much.

Love,
Bill

To finally hear his father's words. What, Willie wondered for the first time, had his father's voice been like? Warm and sure? It must have been. Sure and deep, he decided. A voice that smiled. Everything Grom's voice wasn't.

"But why'd Grom lie about his name?" Willie asked himself. She'd said Peter. "His name's mine. Mine's his."

Willie scanned the letter again. Chest of tools? Mr. Whitehead? His father in Kentucky still didn't make sense. Eagerly, he grabbed the next letter hoping to find the answers.

Dear Kate,

I got lost twice trying to find Whitehead's shop even though it's not far away. The streets here wind all over the place. I can't see for more than two or three blocks most of the time, let alone all the way through town like in Ottawa.

Though I know I saw him when I was little, I wouldn't have recognized Whitehead. He's got the same owlish eyes and thick white mustache that Dr. Obie in history class had, but he's twice as tall and half as fat. So far he isn't much for words. He just pointed to a counter and told me I could put my tools there and to not touch his unless he told me to. He didn't say another word till he stopped for lunch and asked me why I'd come to work with him. I'm not sure he liked my answer, and being put on the spot like that after he'd already said I could come, I'm not sure just what I did tell him. But Kate, you should see the way he works. Today he was finishing up a cherry rocker with the finest curved back you'll ever see. He treated that rocker like he'd just fallen in love. Just watching him work makes playing his errand boy worth the day. The days are going to be long ones, too. He wants me in by seven, and if I get there sooner I can "take breakfast" with them. The day ends when there's nothing left to do, which looks to be never. Mrs. Whitehead's fussing about cold food being bad for the stomach was the only thing that kept me from having to work the night through. I'd guess she's ten years older than your mother and all soft and doughy, with a big gray braid coiled on her head.

It's still hot here and no breeze tonight. . . .

Willie stopped to wipe his forehead and told him–

34

self he'd bring down the window fan before the next letter.

The bed is so old it sways like a horse. We'd both be sliding down into the center and on top of one another all night long. Hmmmmmm? Till soon.

Love,
Bill

Willie was so excited to find that his parents were alive and together, he was torn between reading the letter again and hurrying to read the rest of them. He read it again. And then again. His father's words made the letter feel so alive. Willie still wasn't sure what his father was doing away from his mom, but he felt good knowing that they were in love. He scanned the end of the letter again, then suddenly felt awkward at the image of his parents in bed. As if closing their door, Willie quickly refolded the letter.

"Come on," he told himself as he opened the next letter. "I had to come from *some*place."

August 26, 1964

Dear Kate,
It was so good to find your letter waiting for me tonight. Did you get my postcard yet? I know it isn't as fancy as the ones your pen pals send, but it was the only one I could find that showed more than just buildings. . . .

"Postcard?" said Willie, wanting to see where his father was. He checked, but saw none among the envelopes.

"Later." Willie promised himself he'd search through all the cards he'd already packed in boxes after he'd finished the letters.

I'm sorry you didn't get the promotion. We both know Betsy didn't get the job for just the way she works. Maybe someone else in that department will quit soon. Just remember to not be so shy about speaking out when you know you've got a good idea. Okay?

I know what you mean about not falling asleep. Last night was the first night I've really slept well, and I still woke up wondering where I was. But then it was off to Whitehead's for another day of errands. He still hasn't given me any real work to do. He just says "Not to worry." Mainly he has me taking inventory of his three sheds full of wood. There's a piece of bird's-eye maple that looks like it came from another world.

I just don't know about all of this sometimes. One hour I know it's the right thing to do, and the next I'm convinced it's a big mistake. Especially when I'm still just doing *his* boring work. If my dad . . .

Willie stopped and leaned back. It had been years since he'd really thought of his other grandparents. Since he'd never known who they were or where they lived, he had finally just pretended they'd died before he was born like his grandfather had. Proof they existed made him angry. They'd rejected him as surely as anyone had by never calling or sending a letter.

As best he could, Willie erased them from his thoughts. What mattered most were *his* parents.

If my dad finds out he's paying for me to be an errand boy, he'll lay a brick. But then I never thought he'd help me to come here at all. Maybe your mother was right in saying it was fine for a hobby but no sense for a job.

How's your work going? Mrs. Whitehead asks about you every morning and says you must be very smart to work at a bank and go to school at night. I agree!

The neighbors are as noisy as ever tonight, but at least the radio has some slow dance music on. Last night they had a terrible fight. I've asked the landlady to let me know if any other rooms open up. If I could only afford the one in the upper back corner, I'd have enough room to work on a chair or something of my own at night. Something to fill up the nights alone. Sleep well.

Love,
Bill

P.S. Are any of your mother's mums blooming yet? Mrs. Whitehead has a giant bed of them that looks like a crazy quilt of colors.

Willie felt as if he were swimming fast. So much information in just minutes after so many years of knowing nothing. Each mention of his father missing his mother made him feel happier—even, somehow, more safe. Still, everything was a chain. Knowing his parents were happy made Willie all

37

the more anxious: What was going to happen to make Grom say that his father was better off dead? It was clear from the letters that his father liked Grom.

"She must have been wrong," he said, and reached for another letter. He wasn't about to let Grom spoil the father he'd finally found.

August 29, 1964

Dear Kate,
    It gets so lonely here sometimes. . . .

Willie shifted his weight to his elbows as he looked into Grom's bedroom. She was really gone. He'd been alone now for nearly a month, and missed her as deeply as he'd once wanted to leave her. He thought of calling Libby.

"No," he told himself as he stretched and looked the other way. But no matter where he looked, all he saw tonight were places Grom wasn't.

He gripped the letter tightly like a handle and began to read again.

Rooms full of faces I've never seen and no one to talk to except Whitehead about work (*if* he'll talk) and Mrs. Whitehead about the weather and what it's like in Kansas. It's like you said about the bank. You can talk to them, but not really talk and have them understand.

I wish I could pack up tonight's sky and bring it back to share with you and hold you like we used to do. Remember that night early in the summer when we went out past the park and walked and walked as the stars came out and then just lay in the grass and talked about our dreams? I never thought having a dream come true would make me ache. I like being here and learning wood from Whitehead, but I'm not so sure it was worth all the wishing. Don't mind me. I'm just tired and wish we could talk in person. It helps to know you're there smiling like you did those nights this summer saying, "You know you have to go so go!" You make me feel brave even when I know I'm not. How can some days be minutes and others be years? Till soon. Oh, and thank your mother for her letter.

Love,
Bill

"Why," Willie asked himself, "was Grom writing letters to my father if he was better off dead?"

If he'd thanked her, it must have been a friendly letter. Willie slowly shook his head. Already, his dad's letters were making Grom seem as different as the house seemed with its furniture moved about for the sale.

Willie shoved his chair back and reached into the refrigerator for a Coke. As he turned back to the table, he caught himself smiling. He'd been thinking of his father. He was a real man now with a real job—making chairs—not some impossible movie adventure. His father was doing what he wanted to do instead of just what people told him to do. Willie liked that a lot. He opened his Coke and read on.

September 2, 1964

Dear Kate,

How are your classes going? I still don't understand how anyone can understand calculus. I couldn't even explain what it was to Whitehead the other day. But I'm sure you'll get your usual A.

I'm still watching more than anything else. Thank goodness Whitehead won't give me a test, though everything he says to me feels like I'd better never forget it. He says time is one of the most important things in making anything. That, and helping your hands find eyes of their own. He can work forever all steady and smooth as if his hands *do* know the way without his eyes. And after all his work, he never signs his name to a single chair.

There was a big storm last night with leaves and twigs flying all over the sky. I was out walking as the rain started. The wet winds felt good after so many days of work in the dusty shop and nights thick with sticky air. Feeling the wind blow around my head was the first time I'd really felt alive since getting here. . . .

Willie smiled. Someone else liked the feel of rainy wind. The night a storm had stopped his swimming, he'd enjoyed every minute of the slow walk home. It felt good to know they both liked storms and could have shared such times.

When I got back, I ended up sleeping the soundest of any night since I've been here, too.

40

I showed Mrs. Whitehead the airplane-view postcard you sent since she'd been so curious about Kansas. She just said she couldn't imagine living somewhere that looks "as flat and empty as the moon." Then Whitehead teased her, saying how he didn't know about that and started to talk about all the fun they'd had under the moon till her face turned red and she almost giggled before pretending to be upset. From the looks of their smiles some mornings when I go over for breakfast, I'd guess they're still having some fun under the moon. I miss you so much.

For some reason the neighbors only have the radio on at a normal volume tonight. If they were only playing jazz I could pretend I was home sitting close to you.

Love,
Bill

September 4, 1964

Dear Kate,

How was your week? Mrs. Whitehead sends her best. You should have been here the other morning. The Shoaltner brothers' dog from down the road is just now getting up and around after losing his right hind leg to a tractor. He'll be okay except he doesn't seem to know the leg is gone yet. Twice the other morning he came by to pee on a tree, but when he'd go to hike up his leg, he'd lift the only back leg he's got and go flipping over on his side and spraying everywhere. . . .

Willie laughed out loud.

The more Mrs. Whitehead told us it was mean to laugh, the more we laughed till Whitehead choked on his bacon.

I sure wish you were here so we could talk over the day like we always did at home while cleaning up after supper. All the work he gives me makes the days go fast, but the evenings are twice as long as the clock says they are. With the neighbors fussing at night, I've been going on walks toward the college. The night air gets chilly soon down here.

Tell your mom to just wait and I'll fix the ceiling when I'm back at Christmas. And don't let Betsy eat at you so much. She's just bitchy. Remember how she carried on when you told her I was deferred from the service because of my bad knee? She's always got to be flaunting herself or making fun of somebody else. And *remember*, you look better sleepy in a storm than she does at her best.

Mrs. Whitehead has got her usual growing list of Saturday jobs for me to do so I'd better get to sleep. Best of loving dreams.

Love,
Bill

Willie worked at seeing the three of them, Grom, his mother and his father, talking at the table, all pleased to be together. But he still couldn't imagine his father's face—and when he tried to insert himself in the scene it all began to fade.

September 10, 1964

Dear Kate,

It looks like our letters criss-crossed in the mail. I was glad to hear that Betsy quit even if it was to marry the boss. If you go to the wedding, why don't you trip her for me when she comes down the aisle! . . .

"Jeez," said Willie, and grinned. His father was more fun than any of the ones he'd ever made up. Libby would have liked him too.

"No good," muttered Willie, letting his body sag. None of it mattered. He and Libby were finished, and his dad was dead.

Now that he knew who his father was—what he was like—Willie had something to miss. At the same time the letters were giving him a father, they were also taking that father away.

Willie gave the letter a snap and read on.

Finally Whitehead let me do some real work yesterday. Sort of. He started on a new rocker this week and told me to rough out the upper back slat. Today we spent the whole day steaming and bending slats for the seat. Even if Whitehead sends me packing, I'll be all set to rob banks, as I'm sure I don't have any fingerprints left.

I finally met someone to talk with too—when I was out walking the other night. I stopped to warm up in a little cafe, and since the guy behind the counter and I were the only ones there, we somehow got to talking. He works nights there and takes classes and works at the college during the day. He's studying to be a teacher. I think you'd like him too.

I even got a letter from my dad today. He didn't say much, but wanted to be sure things were going well and said to let him know if I needed to borrow any extra money. I wish he could come and see Whitehead again. Mom and Dad haven't been back here since I was six, when Mother still had relatives down near Richmond.

If the weather is nice on Sunday, Larry (from the cafe)

and I might go hiking around the hills. It'll be good to get away.

Love,
Bill

September 13, 1964

Dear Kate,

It has been a wonderful day! I wish you'd been here. Larry took me hiking in the back hills. My knee only acted up once. It's so different from Ottawa and only a bit like Philadelphia. . . .

"*That's* where," said Willie aloud, thinking of his other grandparents. Then, wanting it not to matter, he told himself, "They had to be somewhere."

Hills and bushes everywhere. We talked and talked and talked and talked. It feels so good to finally know somebody here who isn't my boss. I told Larry that joke you sent about how the cannibal gave his sweetheart a box of "Farmer Fannies" for Valentine's Day. After that we both started telling ALL kinds of jokes. He had one from a book in one of his classes that went on and on about good news and bad news. A man fell out of a plane, which was bad news, but had a parachute, which was good news. But it didn't open, so that was bad news, but there was a haystack below, which was good news. But there was a pitchfork in the hay, which was bad news, but he missed the pitchfork, which was good news. But he also missed the haystack, which was bad news, and on and on and on. He'd have your mother laughing till she'd begin to snort. . . .

44

Willie chuckled to himself. He could remember trying every joke he learned at school in hopes of getting her to laugh like she did on Wednesday nights.

He had to work the late shift at the cafe, so we had supper there and now I'm home getting ready for tomorrow, though it's likely I won't get to do anything but sand. Friday while I was sanding, Whitehead was making a pegged joint. He just kept making a sliver here and another one there on each part, then held them up for a close look and made a final chip. The joint fit perfectly the first time he put the two pieces together. He's got to be the best there is. He keeps saying it's as important to think of the body that will be sitting in the chair as of the wood when you're making it, and it must be true. The chairs he makes feel smooth as skin and like they're a part of my body. I remember when I was little, crawling into the big rocking chair of his in my parents' room just so I could slide my hands back and forth around the curving arms. I'd rock and rock till I felt like I was somewhere else. . . .

Willie was nodding. His own old rocking chair had always been the safest place in the world. In his chair Willie could always think of better times. Even better than that was knowing, now, that he and his father shared the pleasure of rocking alone. It gave him the sense of belonging he'd always missed. Now, rocking and walks in the rain would be times shared with his father.

45

It's warm again tonight, and the campus was full of couples holding hands. By the time I got back here, I was sad and a little jealous (well, maybe a lot!) wishing that we could hold one another safe all night long. Take care, love. 'Bye for now.

Love,
Bill

As he opened the next letter, Willie stood up, walked to the living room and stared at his corner of belongings. The arms and seat of his rocking chair were worn dark and glass smooth from his nights of rocking. The hearts and ivy across the upper back were almost as shiny. Willie smiled, turned off the living-room light, then returned to the table and began to read. Each new letter was like a reunion. The first he'd ever had.

September 17, 1964

Dear Kate,
I didn't know if I was going to make it through work today. Right now I'm so full of coffee I could burst. Larry stopped by last night after he got off work to bring back my sweater he'd borrowed for the hike, and before we knew it we had talked into the middle of the night. . . .

Willie found himself thinking of Libby again. Most of the time it hadn't even mattered what he and Libby had talked about. Talking had given them a reason to stay near one another.

"No point in thinking about all that," he told himself with a shrug. "We're both leaving town."

We talked about everything. He's so easy to talk to, it seems like I've known him for a long time. . . .

Memories of Libby filled Willie's thoughts again.

I wish you two could meet someday. You'd like him.

Did your test go okay? Just keep reminding yourself that after one more semester you'll be able to go after the job you really want at the bank. And get it, too! Then I'll make you a special loan manager's chair when I get back that'll be the best in your bank.

I thought I was full of things to say, but the coffee must be wearing off. My eyes keep sliding shut. Five thirty is going to come far too soon tomorrow morning. 'Bye for now.

Love,
Bill

Willie sat back and smiled as he rolled his shoulders. He was feeling as much like a friend as a son to this man who was writing the letters. He kept forgetting that everything in the letters had already happened *and* ended before he was born.

September 21, 1964

Dear Kate,

How's your hand doing? I'm glad you didn't have to have any stitches. Did your mom give you her usual nurse's lecture on safety again? Whitehead has a long scar on one arm that he says is why he'll never use anything except hand tools. The one and only time he tried an electric saw, he had to get over forty stitches. When I asked him about machines, he said, "Things for people should be made by people. When machines start sitting in chairs, then I'll use machines to make them!"

I think I remember more of my neighbors' fights the next day than they do. Last night they got so loud I spent most of the evening at the cafe helping Larry. He has a sister who works at a bank too, down in a place called Pikeville that's full of millionaires.

Larry said if the noise keeps up at my rooming house, I could move in with him. His place above the cafe has got a couch that turns into a bed I could use. It would save us both money, and with the money I save between now and Thanksgiving there'd almost be enough for you to get a bus ticket down here for a few days. . . .

"That's when!" Willie said to himself. He remembered counting backward in junior high sex ed. class and figuring he'd been conceived when the world was full of turkey and pumpkin pie.

Mrs. Whitehead keeps saying it's going to be one of the most beautiful autumns in a long time. You'll love the mountains and I'd love to see you. Please come. If it weren't for Larry and Mrs. Whitehead, I could fade away from lack of talking. But still, I've got to learn before Whitehead's too old to teach and I'm too scared to try to learn. The mornings are coming all too quickly these days, so I'd better get to bed. Take care.

Love,
Bill

"He talks like building chairs is the most important thing in the world."

Willie dropped the letter in the pile of the ones he'd read. He couldn't imagine this father in the letters running off like Grom had said. How could anyone say this father was better off dead?

4

It seemed impossible that the end Willie had always been told could have grown out of the beginning he was now finding in the letters. The parents in his father's letters had as little in common with Grom's harsh words as they did with Willie's own fantasies.

"Why would Grom have written Dad a letter?" he kept asking himself as he took the next one from the box.

September 26, 1964

Dear Kate,

Work goes on as usual with Whitehead. Hours of work without many words. Just like your mother when she's in her garden. Hours of quiet, then suddenly sharp words. I'm his first apprentice in over ten years, so I guess he's used to quiet. When I asked Mrs. Whitehead if the last apprentice ever came back to visit, her face went tight and she said "NO" in a bitter voice I never expected to hear from her. "At least he's smart enough to not do that!" I don't know what he did or didn't do, but it makes me nervous to speak up very much. Maybe that's why they wanted me to stay at a rooming house instead of with them.

I'm glad everything at the bank is smoothing out now that Betsy's gone. I knew you would make it past the bad times. And if that new woman in charge of investments is as good as you say, maybe she'll be someone you can really talk with about banking instead of just babies and showers and recipes.

Do you still think you can get the time off to come at Thanksgiving? Larry says there'll be plenty of room. We can have his bed. I can't wait to show you Whitehead's shop and the chairs he makes. Once you see them, you'll know why he was the only one I could study with and see what a chair can really be. And don't worry about missing your calculus class. Your professor can tell from your other tests that you study and wouldn't skip a class just out of laziness.

Oh. You'll soon be able to see what Larry and the trees around here look like. Sunday we went walking down by the craft fair and a friend of his took our picture. As soon as it's developed and I get it, I'll send it on to you. . . .

Willie dropped the letter and began digging in the other envelopes. Eager and afraid after all his years of guessing, Willie's hands began to quiver when he found the photograph. One look let him know which man was his father, for Willie saw himself looking back. Still, neither of the men looked old enough to be his father. Though he'd heard of it and told others of his father's youthful death, Willie had always imagined someone as old as Grom.

Willie stared at the picture. He and his father had the same nose. The same guarded eyes. The same oversized hands. Everything in the photograph was a mirror of Willie except that his father had longer hair and a thick scruffy beard.

"She knew!" Willie shouted. Grom had betrayed him again. "She *knew* we looked alike just like she knew we had the same name. She lied."

He leaned wearily against the table. All he could do—all he wanted to do—was stare at his face in the photograph. He wasn't an island after all.

Carefully, he leaned the picture against the side of the shoe box and finished reading the letter.

And just in case you can't tell or have already forgotten, the tall one is me and the handsome one is Larry. 'Bye for now.

Love,
Bill

Again Willie stared into the photograph. Taken before his own birth but not seen till now, it made Willie suddenly feel as if his entire life had been hidden away with the photograph. As he counted the years, Willie tried to imagine his father's face— his own face—dead. His father in the photograph looked only a few years older than Willie was now. The age difference of brothers. At once Willie felt both younger and older than he wanted to be. To be married with a son in just a few years? To die so soon?

October 6, 1964

Dear Kate,
How can you think I've forgotten you? . . .

Willie stopped reading and looked at the last letter's date. A week and a half had elapsed between the letters instead of the usual two or three days.

"He was busy," said Willie in his father's defense.

Except for walking by at night to visit with Larry, I've been doing nothing but working from sunup to past sundown. I'm just not as good at writing letters as you are. You know I think about you all the time. Larry said he was thinking of changing his major to math like you.

Whitehead gave me some maple yesterday with the most beautiful grain. He said "There's enough here to make a chair if you know what to keep and what to cut out. But just enough. Don't cut an inch till you're double-twice sure. Glue's for joints not mistakes." I don't know how I'm supposed to do it. I've stared at that wood and drawn enough sketches and plans to fill up a drawer, but I still don't know what to do. Meanwhile I just keep on sanding on *his* chairs and doing what he says. Yesterday he said he thought I'd better sharpen my tools, so I did even though they were already sharp. At least I thought they were. But when I used them last night, they shaped and cut the wood better than ever before. Now the secret I've got in the works for you will be even better! But since it's bigger than a mailbox, you only get it if you come here *and* if Whitehead doesn't find out.

Just two more weeks and I can move in with Larry. His place looks across the street to some building that's older than all of Ottawa. We went hiking again Sunday. The leaves are already turning here, and we got so busy talking as we walked that we ended up lost for nearly an hour. Talking to him is like thinking to myself, only better. Do you know what I mean? Smooth and easy, like when we floated downstream last summer. . . .

Willie stopped and thought how good the pool water would feel. The one time Libby had gotten him to go to the river, he'd been so restless they'd left in an hour. When he was in water he wanted to move. He thought of going to swim laps right now, but knew he couldn't without reading all the letters.

Best of dreams.

> Love,
> Bill

October 13, 1964

Dear Kate,

Did I ever get it yesterday! Up one side and down the other! I dropped one of Whitehead's favorite chisels as I was rushing to put everything back, and it chipped on a stone. I never thought he could yell so loud. He swore a blue streak and told me that if I had a wooden leg I'd be shit on a stick. . . .

Willie laughed and made a mental note to save that line for the right occasion. Imagining himself saying it, he laughed again, then suddenly stopped. He felt embarrassed for his father at being scolded like that. And that *he'd* laughed.

"Whitehead's the one that's shit on a stick," said Willie, as if his father could hear and might feel better.

I told him I'd sharpen it, but he wouldn't let me touch it. Who knows what he'll say when I get to work this morning. Thank goodness Larry had the night off and didn't have to study much. Just being around him made me feel better. He got to telling me about his relatives that make ours look boring. I laughed all night. Especially about the year they put the turkey that was thawing too fast in a mound of snow on Christmas Eve. When they went to get it Christmas morning, one of its legs had been gnawed off! Larry's dad just told their company how it had been nipped by a fox when a chick and had lived out its fattening days with a wooden drumstick he'd carved to order. Then he even whipped it out as proof, though he'd carved it just that morning. . . .

Willie grinned. "Sounds like something Libby would do."

He thought again for a moment of calling her,

55

but welcomed the excuse of it being too late. He went back to the letter.

. . . Later, after work. Well, it wasn't as bad as I'd feared. Mrs. Whitehead seems to have done a lot to calm him down. All I have to do is make new handles for all my own tools, work all day Sunday, and he'll call it even. I don't get the part about new handles for my tools, but it's better than doing a lot of other things. This afternoon he even told me how he'd cut my piece of maple for the chair. He said it would be tricky but just "listen to the grain and go too slow to suit yourself." Then they both went off to shop in town. It felt good to be in the shop all alone. Like it was mine and I knew what I was doing, even though I didn't. The afternoon went so quickly it seemed they were back in just a few minutes with supper ready. Take care. Till later.

Love,
Bill

October 23, 1964

Dear Kate,
Have you ever felt things you couldn't understand? Or didn't know how to understand? These last few days have run all together like too much glue. Work and more work and finally moving here to Larry's apartment. It's odd to be sharing a place again. Odd to hear him sleeping, but good to be able to talk in the morning like you and your mother always have even if it's only about the weather or things that have to be done.
Fall is certainly here now. The air is musty and the nights will soon be cold enough to wear pajamas. After I carried in the last of my stuff, Larry took me to a

concert of local music to celebrate. The part I liked best was a thing called a hammer dulcimer, where you take long, thin, sticklike hammers and beat what looks like the guts of a tiny piano. The music sounds like a harp only more distant in time. It's sure not jazz, but I still think you'd like it. Maybe there'll be a concert over Thanksgiving. Is your mother still fussing about your coming? I'm sorry it will leave her alone on the holiday. I already wrote to my parents telling them I needed to stay here because you were coming even though Philadelphia isn't that far away. . . .

Willie was filled with envy as his mind flashed full with the image of a table surrounded by noisy relatives. Not once had he had a Thanksgiving dinner with more than just Grom, himself and the turkey. She'd always done more to celebrate the week her lilacs bloomed in April than she had normal holidays. Kneading the base of his neck, Willie scanned the letter again and ground his buttocks against the seat of the kitchen chair. He wasn't used to sitting still so long.

Whitehead has been warming up a bit, and when I told him I was moving to a quieter place, he told me to borrow his truck. Yesterday he even asked me to finish up a joint he'd started.

I'm off now to help Larry find a new suit for his sister's wedding. The one who works in the bank. 'Bye for now. Till soon.

Love,
Bill

November 7, 1964

Dear Kate,

Larry is off to his sister's wedding, so the whole apartment is mine alone. It feels so big and empty, I can't decide where to sit. I really miss his company. Did you get your new dress finished? You always look so good in blue. . . .

Still holding the letter, Willie ran to his box of odds and ends that he'd put near the television. He pulled out the photograph of his mother and himself in the rocking chair.

"I was right! I was right," he said aloud, returning to the kitchen. "Her dress is blue here, too.

"Though," he joked to himself, "it's so short you can barely see the color."

Back at the table Willie took a swallow of his Coke and started to read, then stopped. Delicately, as if connecting an old puzzle, he placed the two photographs beside one another on the table. He tried to imagine his parents in one photograph, but they wouldn't blend together. He and his mother were in color while his father was only black and white. The proportions were also wrong. The heads of his father and Larry were barely half the size of his own and his mother's.

Some days at work I have too much time to think, and I begin to worry about dreams I've had or not had. I worry about being so far away and if there's something wrong with me. Or something wrong with wanting to

58

make chairs more than anything else in the world. At least you and Larry understand that. I took Larry out to see the shop a few nights ago. He didn't know half of what you know about all the files, clamps and chisels, but then he hasn't had to watch me and hear me talk about it for a year like you have. I've been working on your surprise in the evenings, and he keeps teasing me about the chips on the floor. He says I guard my tools like they were the family jewels.

The new handles Whitehead made me make work much better than the ones that came with the tools. I used some scraps of cherry, and they feel like they're a part of my hand.

Thanksgiving and you will both be here before you know it. Wait till you see their house. You've never seen so much beautiful wood and furniture! Bring warm clothes. It's been nippy here. It will be so good to see you and talk with you and hold you while you hold me holding you.

I'm glad your trip gives you an excuse for missing the bank's party at Betsy's new place. Maybe if you tell your mother we'll get her a special souvenir, she won't be so upset about your coming here without her. It would be good to see her too, but certainly not like seeing you! Till soon.

Love,
Bill

Willie began to open the next letter.

"Grom was jealous?"

That meant she must have liked his father a lot.

"Or . . ." he said slowly, "just angry that Mom would leave her alone."

59

November 12, 1964

Dear Kate,

Has it ever been frosty here at night! Somehow, tucked as we are between the hills, the cold seems to settle in sooner here and stay longer into the day. Soon it will be dark when I walk out to the Whiteheads'. We're invited to their Thanksgiving dinner. Mrs. Whitehead said it's just not right to not be at a big dinner that day. . . .

Who cares? thought Willie. Hearing someone say that Grom's Thanksgiving dinners for two were wrong made him bristle. Even though he agreed, Willie wasn't about to let a stranger speak against Grom.

And will she ever have a big one. Three of her sisters and their families, and four of Whitehead's brothers and sisters and their families, are coming. Plus the Shoaltner brothers from down the road. That is, until she invites some more. Whitehead just smiles and shakes his head saying, "It keeps getting bigger the older we get." The best I can tell, they never did have any children of their own. Neither of them spends much time speaking of the past.

I'll try to meet you at the bus depot. But just in case I can't get away from work or the bus is early, I'll send you a map to the apartment. It's just a few blocks. And since Larry will be gone for Thanksgiving after all, there's no need to bring pajamas!

Willie grumbled, pretending to be indifferent, but smiled. He knew the letter and the trip *and* lack of pajamas were all leading up to his beginning. His birth and part in the family.

Well, I'd better get back to work. Whitehead has an order for six matching high-back chairs that somebody wants for Christmas. It's hard to work as fast as you can and still as slow and careful as you need to. Somehow Whitehead does it, though. If only I could too. Take care and see you soon. Smiles to your mom.

Love,
Bill

November 30, 1964

Dear Kate,
I hope your trip back went better than the ride coming out and that you didn't have to hear another drunk sing for thirty miles. In some ways it's hard to believe you were ever here. . . .

Willie slowly ran his fingers over his head and grinned. He'd been conceived between the two letters.

"One turkey baby on his way!"

Everything's back to the same again. Long days of sanding and oiling and running around for Whitehead. I'll be glad to see Christmas come and go, *and* have all these chairs done and gone. Until then there's no time for much else. It tires me just to think of it, but this whole autumn seems to have worn me down. I'm sorry I wasn't very romantic for you. Who would ever have thought I'd be so tired we'd only be able to make love once? We'll just have to catch up later. . . .

Willie anxiously read the last lines again. He felt vulnerable knowing he'd almost not been started at all. Now that he knew both their faces, he tried to imagine his parents in bed, but he kept remembering himself and Libby instead.

"Past," he announced, and read on.

Whitehead really liked you. He says you've got a heart of earth strung tight with spunk. . . .

Willie laughed at the corny words, but still smiled with pride for his mother.

I thought he'd be upset if he knew about your rocker. Especially if he knew I'd made it from his scrap pile. But after you left, he asked me what your rocker looked like and if you'd liked it. When I told him about the carving on the back, he just shook his head and said, "Sounds pretty, but a good chair don't need any flowers for help. It's beautiful when it's comfortable. That makes it touched and used a lot." That may be, but I still like the hearts and ivy. . . .

"Hearts and ivy . . . mine!" said Willie. "*He* made it."

His voice kept rising in excitement and anger.

"All those years. He made it . . . and she knew it.

"Damn you!" he said as he remembered when Grom had tried to throw it out. "DAMN YOU!"

Willie stared toward her empty room.

"Maybe *you're* the one," he called out as his voice began to crack, "that's better off dead."

Once again Willie felt as if she'd whacked his world in the back of the knees. Who knew what else she knew and had never told him. By not giving him the memories of all that he and his father shared, it seemed that Grom killed his father as surely as whatever really had. He shook his head. She'd never even told him how his father had died.

Intent on rejecting Grom's world, Willie returned to the letter that was giving the truth and began to read aloud.

Some days chairs are the only thing I think I even begin to understand. My love to you.

Love,
Bill

"Maybe she didn't know," Willie whispered as he tried to fill the vacuum of silence that had followed his charge she was better off dead.

But he knew she had. "How could she *not* have known?"

December 14, 1964

Dear Kate,

We had the first snow of the season last weekend. It was beautiful. All wet fluffy whiteness clinging to the tree branches. Forgive me for falling behind in my letters. These two weeks have been nothing but work and confusion, but at least work is the one thing that never changes on you. If you think your mother would like one of those sewing baskets we saw to replace your dad's old cigar box she uses for crocheting, let me know. I'll try to get her one for Christmas. I promise to write a real letter soon.

Love,
Bill

"So that's why she guarded it and fussed if she couldn't find it," thought Willie. "Her cigar box was Grandpa's before he died. Probably Mom's in her desk was his, too."

Willie arched his back until it popped. He felt uneasy that the letter had been so short after so long a time. The next one was just as brief.

December 16, 1964

Dear Kate,

Of course Christmas back in Ottawa would be terrific. We'd always planned on that. I was already planning to ask Whitehead if I can get extra time off once the big order is done this week. He'll be in a better mood then. If my parents give me money like last year, I might even have enough for a plane ticket. They *still* think I should go visit them. I'll sleep all the way on the plane so I won't be too tired to do important things all night once I get to Ottawa. I'm off to mail this on the way to work. More news soon. Love and long deep kisses.

Love,
Bill

"He's as horny as the guys on the swim team," Willie said to himself. At least the letter was a good one.

December 19, 1964

Dear Kate,

I can't leave at all now. They need me around here. I'm sorry I haven't been writing as often as you. But you know I want the best for you. I'll call on Christmas. Mrs. Whitehead says she doubts there'll be more than four flakes of snow. There's so much to say. If only everything could be as clear as today's cold air.

Love,
Bill

Willie took a fast breath. The letters were quickly becoming a maze.

"Why doesn't he just *tell* old Whitehead he's going to Ottawa and go? And what's 'so much to say'? He doesn't even sound upset about missing Christmas."

Willie began to read the last letter again, then stopped. Whatever was going on—whatever was going wrong—was in the letters to come. He pulled the next one out of its envelope as quickly as he could.

December 26, 1964

Dear Kate,

I'm so sorry. Sorry and afraid. I couldn't call you yesterday. I mean I could, but I couldn't. . . .

Willie turned away from the letter.

"No," he ordered as his skin flashed hot and he

65

steadied both feet flat to the floor. It was as if the morning he'd woken knowing Grom had died was happening all over again. That airless moment when he knew that something vital had changed and that there was no going back.

He snatched the box off the table and by instinct went straight to his rocking chair. With the box in his lap Willie rocked as hurriedly as he finished the letter.

I'm not sure what to say except that I wish you well and want only the best for you. Sometime there will be so much to say and I'll know where to begin. Forgive me. Please.

> Love,
> Bill

Willie tore open the next envelope. All he could think of was Grom saying "better off dead."

January 10, 1965

Dear Kate,
I'll be fine. Please don't call the Whiteheads anymore. It frightened them. If I sound confused it's because I'm *not* confused for the first time in my life. If only I could write this and not hurt you like I know I already have. I love you, Kate, but I can't be your husband any-more. . . .

Willie held in his breath. The dream the letters had started—the family story he'd always wanted to hear—was splintering deep inside his chest.

"No," he said, and sucked in air. "You're home-sick. You missed her. You wanted to *sleep* with her."

Everything was derailing no matter how slowly Willie reread the words.

I can't love you the way you should be loved by a husband. I thought I could, but I can't. I never can, though I love you as my truest friend. You're the first one who believed in my dreams as much as I did. It's all chicken-shit scary, but it's also like breathing deeply for the very first time. And I like it. Remember when I wrote and asked you if you'd ever felt things you didn't understand or were afraid to feel? Well, I have all my life. It's just that now, I mean— Damn. This is so scary to say out loud. I love you, you have to believe that, like a friend, my best friend, but not like a lover. I love men. I'm attracted to men. . . .

Willie felt himself sinking. Too numb to fight against it. Too lost to feel any anger. He had no defenses for this.

"How can you?" he pleaded as his whole face burned. "How can you know?"

For a moment he wanted to drown in a giant wave and be done with it.

"Damn you," he said. His voice was hoarse now. "You love her. You . . . I thought you'd . . ."

Willie had no idea how long he'd been sitting when he finally looked at the letter again. His own father was one of *them*. Though it felt like he was swimming a losing race, Willie read on as he began to rock again. More than ever he had to know the story's end.

I guess I always have been, but buried deep, the way all those years you cut and flattened your curly hair. . . .

"What the hell does curly hair have to do with being queer?" Willie yelled. He was rocking so quickly, the chair was inching sideways.

It was there and you knew it, but you pretended it wasn't because everyone told you it was ugly. You hid it so long, you even forgot what you looked like with your natural curls. There's sense in all of this. I'm just no good at explaining things I barely understand myself. Maybe you already felt some of this. Kids at school always teased me like they already knew. And it looks like they did. Long before I did. . . .

"Arnie," whispered Willie. There'd been jokes about him since the fifth grade, when someone caught him staring in the locker room.

As Willie slowed his rocking, the father he'd longed for and had finally found in the letters withered in his mind. It seemed he had even less now than he had when he'd known nothing about his father at all.

68

Everything but the letters and the rhythm of the rocking disappeared as Willie began to read again. Then he stopped dead, stood up and looked at the rocker.

"Grom was right."

Not wanting to sit, Willie finished the letter as he aimlessly walked from room to room.

I used to wish I had polio or was blind so I'd have some reason for feeling so different from everyone else. God, Kate. I never meant to lie to you. I didn't lie to you. I always told you what I believed myself. I told you I loved you and I did. I *do*. It was me I lied to, and as long as I did, the truths I told could never be fully true. I see that now. The way I did lie to you was by not being able to give you the full passion that you gave me. You deserve the best, Kate, and I can't be the best for you. I lied by thinking I *was* giving you all there was to give and share, but I was wrong. Maybe you already sense that too. I couldn't and didn't even know what was missing, because I'd never felt it coming from inside me. I wish I could be the husband and lover you deserve and thought you had. But I can't.

I don't know what to do except be as honest as I know how, though I thought I was doing that before. But if I could lie to you, Kate, I wouldn't be writing this letter. You've got to believe me. Please write back. I need to hear something from you. I need you and care for you as the friend you were before we were married, were while we were married and still are. How can I prove I don't mean to hurt you? Please forgive me. Please write.

Love,
Bill

"They'll work it out," Willie told himself, though the muscles in his stomach refused to agree. "They have to work it out. She kept the letters."

January 20, 1965

Dear Kate,
    I've told you all I already know. I didn't trick you into getting married *or* coming here at Thanksgiving. And if I wanted to use you, why would I be telling you all this now? I didn't lie when we got married any more than you did. We just didn't know all the truth. There's got to be a difference. . . .

Willie glanced at the two photographs on the table—at the two men smiling in one and his mother and himself smiling only inches away.

It doesn't make any difference if there is somebody else. It's me that's making the change. No, not even a change. An overdue truth. There's no contest between you and anybody else. It's just me against me. Or finally me NOT against me.
    Please let me know the truth about what's going on. I got a letter from your mother yesterday that cut like a knife. Are you really pregnant like she says? You've got to tell me. You've got to let me make things right, though I'm not sure what that would be. At least I could come back to Ottawa for a while and help pay the bills. Tell people in Ottawa anything you want. Tell them lies. Tell them the truth. They'll all feel sorry for you anyway. Just let me know if you're pregnant or not.

Bill

Willie nervously wiped the sweat on his forehead over the top of his head. They were talking about him now. He was finally a part of the family story just as the story was starting to split and sink.

"Damn."

January 28, 1965

Dear Kate,

I don't need a doctor. I'm fine. You've got to believe me. I think I was so tired *because* I was worrying about all of this. I didn't choose for things to be this way. It just happened. Like when you and I met at the demonstration. Yes. I do love Larry. But I'm not choosing him over you. And I didn't sleep with him before you came for Thanksgiving. I couldn't. He wanted to and I guess I wanted to, but I didn't want to want to. I didn't. . . .

"So that means you are *now*." Willie flipped the picture of his father and Larry facedown on the table. It was more comfortable to think of him dead than kissing another man.

I didn't. That's why I wanted you to come. I'm not rejecting you. You have to believe me. I'm just accepting me, and Larry is a part of me now. A part of my world. You know I'd try being different if I thought I could. I just can't. I've already tried—all my life. To stay married now would be a lie, and I've already lied to myself for too long. I don't want any lies anymore. . . .

"So lie!" ordered Willie. "You were happy when you lied before."

I'm just so glad you're not really pregnant. . . .

"But she *is*," argued Willie. "She is with *me*!"
He tried to read on, but his eyes kept darting.
"She's lying me out of his life—she's erasing me. And she *knows* that he'd come back for me. He said so."
Willie felt as desperate as he was helpless to change what he read. His mother, not Grom, had been the one who had taken his father away. His mother had lied.
"At least Grom tried to tell him that I was alive. That I *was*."

And, if you're so mad at me because you think I lied, then why did you tell your mother I was cheating with another woman? The truth won't change.

Bill

Breathing slow but shallow breaths, Willie took the next letter and stood up from the table. Then, before taking a step, he turned the picture of himself and his mother facedown too. He wished he could erase all the facts, all the lies. He thought for a moment of burning all the letters. But he knew he couldn't, at least not yet. As hard as it was, the storm of the letters' facts and lies was still better than the lifeless silence he'd always had. And burning them wouldn't make him forget.

"Mom read them all," he told himself as he let the back screen door slam shut behind him.

The air outside was as still as in the kitchen, but the wet flower beds freshened the heat with their earthy smells of living. He tried to reread the letter he still had in his hand, but the night was too dark.

"Why can't she . . . why couldn't she . . . tell him that I was alive?"

Not once had he ever thought his father's story—or his mother's—would be so simple or so hard.

"Unless she didn't want him to be my father." Willie was eased by his new scrap of logic. "Why *would* she give me a queer for a dad?"

Willie gazed across Grom's flower beds, then headed for the house. This time he caught the screen door with his hand and closed it gently.

"Mom read them all," he told himself again as he sat back down at the table. "If she kept them, they *must* have worked it out."

February 1, 1965

Dear Kate,

What good would talking on the phone do? Besides, I can't use the Whiteheads' phone without them hearing. There's no phone where I live, and I'm not going to stand at a pay phone with people walking by while I try to say the same things I've already written. Larry didn't trick me into anything. And neither of us pretends to

73

be the woman. Being with Larry is to *not* pretend anything anymore. Knowing Larry has helped me learn the
truth about what I wasn't able to share with you. I'm
sorry for the hurt, but not for the truth. If you ever did
love me, you'd know that I wouldn't just decide to hurt
you. You've got to believe me. The hardest part right
now is that I need my best friend more than ever and
you're my best friend.

With love,
Bill

Willie reached back to the photograph of his
father, slowing as he touched it. Uncertain of whom
he would see or wanted to see, he turned it faceup
and stared again. Both men were smiling. When he
turned his own picture over, his mother was smiling
as well as he himself. It seemed like they were all
wearing masks.

February 6, 1965

Dear Kate,

I'm doing what I'm doing because I *do* love you. And
because I finally like me. You can't really believe that
this has anything to do with your looks or brains. You're
wonderful! And why would either of our mothers have
anything to do with it?

I just want to live what I feel, like you do. All I'm
trying to do is live the truth. Why does that have to be
so hard?

My love to you,
Bill

"Why does it have to be so friggin' hot?" said Willie as he moved to unstick himself from the plastic of the kitchen chair.

He thought again of getting the window fan, but only reached around behind himself to pull a fresh Coke out of the refrigerator.

February 21, 1965

Dear Kate,

I believe that you want to help me, but really helping me means believing what I say. Divorce me and find a man who can love you like Whitehead loves his wife and have the family you dream of having someday. . . .

"She wanted me."

Tell the lawyer I'll sign anything he wants me to. Tell him whatever you want to. Tell anything that makes it easier on you. People will talk no matter what. Tell them the truth about me like you finally did to your mother.

"Grom knew," whispered Willie, as the words "unfit to be a father" echoed in his head. "And didn't want me . . . to have to know."

As quickly and intensely as he'd wanted to yell at her for lying about his father's name and face, Willie wanted, now, to smile and give her papery hand a grateful squeeze for keeping it a secret from everyone.

75

March 28, 1965

Dear Kate,

Since you've completely ignored my questions about the divorce papers, I'm guessing that your mother has been throwing out my letters before you get home from work. I hope you'll get this one by my sending it to the bank.

I'll put in all the money I have to help pay for the lawyer, and as soon as my dad's next check arrives I'll send it on to pay for the rest. I've never known how to tell them anything important, and after they carried on about how we were too young to marry, I don't want them to think they were right. They weren't. Knowing you is one of the best things I've ever done.

I finally told the Whiteheads about us. I had to say something after your phone calls. They both looked sad and said we should have kept trying to work it out. Then they tried to feed me till I thought I'd burst. I was surprised at how frightened I felt when I told them. I hated to disappoint them. I told them you'd met some-body who could give you a much better life than I could. And it's not a lie, because I know you will.

Yours,
Bill

5

Willie sat toying with the next letter. He knew he would read it and all the rest, but still wanted to prove he felt no rush. As far as he could reason, knowing wouldn't really change a thing. They'd already died and left him.

May 25, 1965

Dear Kate,

Thanks for your last letter. It means a lot. If only everyone knew how special you are. My dad's been gone for over a week, but it still feels like he's here. If only he could be more like you. He's always got to be in control of everything. Nothing can be right for him unless he put it that way. . . .

"Grom," said Willie automatically, as if tapped with a reflex hammer.

He complained because I hadn't told them earlier, then complained about such upsetting news and how it would hurt my mother. He went on and on about the sacrifices he made when he first married my mom and on and on. For him a sacrifice meant having only five suits instead of ten. It was hard to explain when I couldn't tell him the truth. I didn't know how. I know he won't be able to understand. My mother would want me cured by a shrink like you first did. And my dad would cut off my allowance to study here. He did seem to like Larry, though, but then, Larry even made me feel like we were nothing but friends all the time my father was here.

At least working with wood remains itself. More and more it seems like nothing can show the truth about a person better than what they've made with their hands. Just looking at Whitehead's chairs and Mrs. Whitehead's garden tells you as much about them as their words ever will. Last night as we walked around after supper, Whitehead began naming trees just by the sounds of their leaves in the night breeze. When I told Mrs. Whitehead, she just said, "Sure as anything he's got sap instead of blood." It's so good to watch them together.

I'm glad you've been going out some lately. Next time your mother starts carrying on about you being out too late, just try some bourbon. Larry has a little every night before bed. He says it files down his worries to where he can barely feel them.

The bad news is that he has to be gone all summer to work on his family's farm. He says he doesn't want to go, but it's all he talks about. I'll be moving in with the Whiteheads while he's gone. It'll save me money and keep me busy helping in their summer garden. Well, I'd better close now. I promised I'd type Larry's term paper tonight.

> Take care.
> With love,
> Bill

Dear Kate,

I'm sorry I'm so late to answer your last two letters. Not being sure what else to do, I just keep working later and later every night. Being at the Whiteheads' full-time isn't really so different from before except now I can hear Whitehead snore (like a power saw!) and sometimes catch Mrs. Whitehead without her teeth. The funniest times are during supper. Whitehead always says his eyes are too tired to read the paper, so she tells him the news and *Gasoline Alley* and *Alley Oop.*

Why would you think I'd be jealous? I'm glad that you've been dating Jake. Did you meet him at school? Besides getting out, it must be good to get away from your mother now that she's home all day long during summer vacation. And if she can't handle the truth when she asks for it, then tell her something she wants to hear. What you do when you stay late at Jake's place is your business. Just as long as you and Jake know what's true between the two of you, what difference does it make *what* you tell her? . . .

"He told her to lie," whispered Willie. Then he nodded slowly in recognition. His mother was lying to Grom just like he had so many nights when he'd gone swimming.

Willie began to read again, then stopped and drew back his head. The story he was piecing together through the letters was impossible. He'd forgotten that *he* was now part of the story too.

"She was seven months pregnant with me," argued Willie. "Seven months. She can't be sleeping with Jake. Why would she say she was when she wasn't?"

As for me there's still no word from Larry. Maybe a walk in the warm breeze out to the old shed where some bourbon awaits will ease another night. I can't understand why he hasn't written.

Love to you,
Bill

" 'Love, Bill . . . Love, Bill,' " mocked Willie as he refolded the letter.

He let his tired eyes rest on the familiarity of Grom's "Walk with Jesus" calendar that still showed July. Already those days seemed years away. Why couldn't things have stayed like they were?

"Don't write," Willie wished of Larry. "Maybe *then* he'll start being normal again."

His own life told Willie that his parents hadn't remarried. But married or not, he didn't want *his* father to be gay when he died.

The next envelope only held a postcard. Willie read it quickly without looking at its picture.

July 3, 1965

Dear Kate,

Here's a postcard for your collection. I found it at a flea market when I took Mrs. Whitehead over to sell her extra tomatoes. Thanks for your card. Larry finally sent a note, but all he wrote about was his lazy teenage brother. He must be afraid someone else will read his letters. I'm going to ask for time off to go visit him. What with the heat, everything here is at a slower pace— except the weeds. So I think Whitehead will let me. Take care and stay as cool as you can.

As ever,
Bill

P.S. How are your mom's beloved glads doing this year? They're one of the few flowers Mrs. Whitehead doesn't grow. Happy Birthday, too!

"Even back then . . ." said Willie, and softly smiled.

August 1, 1965

Dear Kate,

As always I owe you letters. The last month has been nothing but questions without answers. You're so lucky to have met Jake. Larry has only written twice all summer even though we promised to write once a week. The second note was only to tell me not to come visit. He said he wasn't much of a letter writer, but still. I've already found us a new apartment, but we both have to start deciding where we'll go after he graduates in December. I've got to figure out how to tell Whitehead I'm leaving. But I can't tell him about Larry and me.

At least when I'm busy in the shop I feel more at ease. Sometimes when I'm filing or sanding, it feels like I could slide right into the wood and disappear. Hours feel like minutes and everything feels in its place. But even Whitehead thinks I've been working too much. The hard part is that I can't even tell anyone that I miss Larry. He could be hurt or killed in an accident and nobody would think to let me know because we can't let anyone know we care.

My check finally arrived from Dad, but so did his note saying that he and Mom are coming to visit in September. Wish me luck.

My love to you,
Bill

October 3, 1965

Willie stopped at the date. October 3, 1965. It had been written long after August 7, the day he was born.

"But he died *before* I was born," Willie said in defeat.

He had wanted the letters to tell him what Grom never had, but he'd never expected such confusion. Each letter only made the past seem muddier.

"But if he wrote a letter after I was born . . ."

Willie glanced at the pile of letters still in the shoe box.

"If he wrote *letters* after I was born, maybe he's still alive." His thoughts were spinning ahead. "But where? Berea? What made Grom think he was dead?"

More questions. Once again he had a new reason to finish all the letters.

October 3, 1965

Dear Kate,

I'm sorry I've been so long to write. Things got so bad they could only get better, but it's taken forever to

believe any better times were coming. Your letters and
making a new rocker were the only good things about
September.

My parents came to visit three weeks ago. I was going
to try to tell them, but I couldn't. Besides, there didn't
seem much point to it since Larry had gone before they
got here. So you don't have to worry about me giving
up chair making for him after all. Actually he never came
back. . . .

"Good." Willie said it as quickly and surely as if
bolting a door.

He came back to Berea, but didn't tell me till I saw him
at the market. I stood there trying to get him to tell me
what was wrong, but he acted like nothing had ever
happened between us. How can he just erase everything? I finally left work sick yesterday. I just couldn't
keep from crying, and there's no way to explain it to
anyone around here. I can't even lie and say he died,
like your mother did when your dad left her for that
woman in Kansas City. At least she could say they'd
been married and together. . . .

Willie closed his eyes. He'd found out too many
lies to be surprised by another. But to *never* have
known that Grom had been divorced.

"Grom . . . no wonder you never talked about
him."

Willie was gradually realizing that everyone who'd
left him had left her, too, plus her husband.

"Grom?" If she'd lied about her husband dying,

thought Willie, then she could have lied about his father's death.

Willie was about to shake his head at her lies when he remembered he'd done the same thing about his father's parents. As long as he'd pretended they were dead, it was easier to forget them and how they had ignored him.

Everything here feels as numb as my hands after sanding all day. When I told the Whiteheads Larry needed to move in with a cousin (so I lied), they invited me to move back in with them. At least *they* want me.
'Bye for now.

Love,
Bill

By habit Willie opened the next envelope and began to read, but his thoughts kept returning to Grom and his grandfather who'd left her.

Why had Grom kept his grandfather's cigar box if he'd left her? And why had he gone, anyway?

"Grandpa Jerk," he said in disgust. Willie didn't want to care why he'd gone away. His grandfather had left Grom, and being left was always the same. It made you feel as if you didn't exist. Like people could look and not see you. He'd felt it. So had his mom. Willie glanced at the black-and-white photograph.

"Dad, too," he whispered, remembering the recent letters.

Dear Kate,

I just need to talk. I went to see Larry this afternoon.
Damn him! All that he'd say was that his family would
never understand and that he couldn't disappoint them.
I tried to talk with him, but he just said he guessed he
didn't know how to love anyone, then walked away. He
just walked away. . . .

Willie stopped reading. He'd wanted Larry gone,
but now found himself angry at his leaving. Larry
had shut his father out with silence just like Grom
had always done. As he read the letter again, he
suddenly felt exposed. He could hear himself having made much the same excuses to every girl who'd
gotten serious. He'd told Libby, too.

"After . . ." said Willie. "I just walked away that
night at the swimming pool.

"But that was different," he said as he returned
to the letter. "It *was*." He'd *only* been protecting
himself.

It was as if I was standing on a mountain and the
mountain suddenly vanished. When he went home for
the summer, he told me he wished he could stay with
me. He said he'd always be with me even if he had to
be miles away. How can he change his feelings so fast?
How could I believe him? And if things can change so
fast, why can't they change back again? Sometimes I
begin to wonder if I imagined it all.

To see her face, I think Mrs. Whitehead knows how
I feel about Larry, but she won't say a thing. Right now

I'd rather she didn't know. When she knows but won't speak of it, it all seems twice as forbidden. I hate the silence. Sometimes I feel like I could explode from not being able to say what's really wrong. Or even right. Me knowing who I am. I'm sorry I've gone on so long without even asking how you are. You know I hope you're doing well and that all is well with you and Jake.

Take care,
Bill

November 4, 1965

Dear Kate,

If I wasn't so glad that you're happy, I would be jealous of you and Jake. I like hearing about your good times together, but it still makes me sad. . . .

"What about *me?*" asked Willie as if his mother could hear him. "You can write him about boyfriends, but not about me?"

It hurt deeply enough that Grom hadn't told Willie about his father, but it hurt even more that his mother hadn't told his father that Willie was even alive. Reading the letters made it seem like he'd never been born.

. . . but it still makes me sad. I know you said don't ask such questions about how and why Larry changed because there aren't any answers. But I don't see why. There have to be answers. There are always answers. And if I knew some of the answers, maybe I could help Larry understand and change his mind again. . . .

86

Willie let his neck go limp. If only the letters would twist over again, turning everything he'd read so far into another lie and give him an easier truth—give him an answer that would stay the same.

"Just let my dad *change*," he bargained with himself. "At least that. Like Larry."

He leaned back against the chair, glad to feel its support.

Mrs. Whitehead's already started baking for Thanksgiving dinner. Even more food than last year. I just now realized that everybody will be asking about you. They liked you, and I can't *not* go since I'm living here. I'll think of something to tell them. Or maybe the Whiteheads will tell them ahead of time. It'll still be better than going home. I told my parents that Whitehead was under the weather and couldn't spare me. This really feels like home anyway.

Take care and enjoy your holiday times with Jake. And watch out for one-legged turkeys!

As ever,
Bill

December 15, 1965

Almost a year since he told her, thought Willie as he read the date. The year of confusion and pain, condensed into this one night of reading, had left him weary. By now the letters had pulled him through too many changes to still be exhilarating. His body felt as heavy as after swimming laps, but with none of the joy.

December 15, 1965

Dear Kate,

Best of holly wishes to you. This year's as busy and buried under work as last year was slow. We've got three special orders for Christmas. But we did have fun last Sunday. Somehow Mrs. Whitehead talked Whitehead into visiting her Sunday school class as Santa Claus. He had so much fun, he kept the suit on till midafternoon. The last thing he did before he took it off was give me a little package with one of his favorite chisels inside. He could have given me gold and it wouldn't have meant as much. . . .

Willie smiled. He thought how good it would have been to spend the next holiday with the three of them in Berea. Like a family.

I'm going home to Philadelphia for a week. Actually I've got to more than I want to. My parents are really after me to see my brother. I'm sure he couldn't care less. I haven't seen him since I started to school in Ottawa. I just hope there aren't other relatives there. It's so hard to just sit there and smile when they tease and ask about girlfriends. The last thing I want to hear about is all my brother's girlfriends and how his classes at Columbia are so easy for him. You know how Mother thinks he can do no wrong. The trouble is, he usually doesn't. Wish me luck. Best of wishes to you and Jake.

With love,
Bill

February 6, 1966

Dear Kate,

Your New Year's letter all but bounced off the walls as I read it. You make this Keith sound like a Paul Newman and Albert Schweitzer rolled into one. Who cares if he's ten years older? Does he have a brother with a secret? Maybe *I* should start hanging around the jazz section of the record store. . . .

"Don't they *ever* give up?" Willie joked. He wanted to laugh but could only wag his head like a tired parent. "Why bother?"

Your Valentine's weekend trip to Kansas City sounds wonderful. I'm glad you'll finally get to hear Dave Brubeck play in person. I can almost hear your mother worrying about what the neighbors will think. Even though the only way they'll find out is by her telling them.

My Christmas trip home was okay, though every other time a beautiful woman came on television, they'd ask me who I was dating. I'd just say "No one. Work takes too much time these days, and besides there really isn't anyone there to date." Which is more truth than lie and keeps all of us comfortable. Or at least me in charge of how they treat me. I know my private life is mine to keep private just like yours is from your mom, but not telling them makes me feel like a liar. And not having the option makes me feel trapped. . . .

Willie's eyes stuck to the word "trapped." He'd felt trapped by Grom when she wouldn't tell him the truth about his father. His father felt trapped

89

because he couldn't tell people the very same truth. And now Willie felt trapped by knowing it.

Anyway, it was good to return to Berea and the Whiteheads. They feel more like family than Philadelphia does now. Here things just seem to fall into place. Work and chores. Food and sleep. I can end up going for days without seeing other people and I don't miss them. Even when it gets tricky, nothing feels better than quietly sanding and shaping a chair.

Since the Whiteheads are in bed by nine, I've got several hours to myself every night. I've started carving wooden copies of Mrs. Whitehead's shell collection. So far I've got four done with fifteen to go. I'm saving her favorite to do last, when I'll be doing my best carving. It's one of the plainer ones in color—you remember, she showed it to you when you were here—the one that has two halves that fit together like a heart.

Well, I'd better close for now. I can smell breakfast cooking and I'm not even out of bed yet. 'Bye for now.

As ever,
Bill

P.S. I know it's your business, but what happened to Jake? You two seemed to be so close.

Willie smiled softly with the warmth of the letter. Making chairs was sounding more and more like swimming. Except, admitted Willie to himself, he had nothing to share after swimming laps.

Without thinking, Willie pulled the photograph of his father and Larry near him again. Then, as carefully as if matching torn pieces, he placed the one of himself and his mother over the first, blocking out Larry. Now all three faces in his family were smiling at once as if they were happy together. Father, mother, son and the family rocking chair.

He was too pleased with his self-made family to care what had happened to Jake or what's-his-name. Willie had already forgotten the new guy's name.

March 1, 1966

Dear Kate,

I'm glad your trip with Keith went well. He does sound special. Sometimes you and I are more alike than we remember. Your letters about Jake *were* making me envious. I was thinking about making up a boyfriend to see if I could make Larry jealous enough to come back. Now you tell me you were doing exactly that by making up Jake. . . .

Willie stared at her photograph that still overlapped his father's. Grom hadn't lied this time, *she* had. Again. How could she lie about having a boyfriend to get his father back *and* lie about not having a baby—him—to keep his father away?

Willie sighed with a half laugh. It was all beginning to seem like Larry's old joke of good news and bad news with the news of each letter shifting the story from good to bad. Bad to good and truth to lie. The trick, figured Willie, as he shook his head at the mess, was to stop with a good news and ignore the next bad. But as often as not he couldn't tell good from bad till the next change came.

"Gettin' only makes you want," said Willie as he remembered Grom's flat words. "You're better off without. She did her best and all I've found is bad."

As he began reading again, Willie promised himself he'd finish the letters and try his best to forget them all. He'd leave them behind like they'd left him.

"Except . . . " he told himself as he looked at the photographs, "Dad didn't really leave me. He never got the chance."

As he returned to the letter Willie softly said "Dad" once again.

I'm glad it didn't work. You're happy with Keith and I've got to realize that Larry's too scared to be with me. Besides, what could last if it was based on a lie?

All in all things have been good around here. Last week was sad and somehow joyful at the same time— at least for me. One of the Shoaltner brothers on the neighboring farm died in his sleep. He was only 68. You remember them from Thanksgiving? When I ran over after David called, I found him holding George's hand in the big double bed. He was crying so hard he couldn't stop. When David saw me come in, he kissed his brother's hand and said, "Promise me you'll see that I'm buried next to him. Please." And then with pride said, "Forty years we got to be together." He told me how they had combined their names to make Shoaltner when they'd moved to Berea saying they were brothers even though they weren't. I couldn't help but cry with him, and held him as he held his "brother" until the ambulance came. Forty years of secrets. I'm so glad I was the one who got there first. Do you think he could tell I was safe to tell? Forty years of love together. Take care, dear Kate, and enjoy your spring with Keith.

Love,
Bill

P.S. I'm glad you could tell Keith the truth about me.

"Forty years," said Willie. They'd been together twice as long as he'd known Grom. Over twice his life. Why, he wondered as he opened the next envelope, did the truth always change when someone died?

April 28, 1966

Dear Kate,

Finally I have a letter for you with good news. Last week we planted three dozen new trees around the farm. A dozen each of cherry, maple and walnut. As we finished up, Whitehead said they were for the best chairs I'd ever make. That turned out to be his way of asking me to stay on as his partner. And you can be sure I said YES! . . .

"He did it." Willie was grinning with pride.

Mrs. Whitehead was so certain of my answer that she'd cooked a celebration supper. I don't think I've ever lived a spring this fine. Things feel solid and good in a truer way than ever before. I've been . . .

"But if . . . " Willie had been filling his mind with images of their celebration—himself included—when

93

he realized that it wouldn't have been such a special time if his father had known he had a son.

"If he'd come back to Ottawa for me," Willie explained to himself, "Whitehead could never have asked him to stay on as a partner."

I've been going over every few evenings to help David Shoaltner with chores and listen to him reminisce about his "brother." His eyes shine like polished cherry when he talks about George. I want so much to tell him I understand, but I'm not sure he remembers what he said that day when he was so upset. He hasn't mentioned it since.

Did I tell you my brother's getting married? She's a real New Yorker and thinks it's "just so sweet to have a relative off in the mountains making chairs the old-fashioned way." What I'd like to do is send them a broken lawn chair as their present. The wedding will be in New York. When I told the Whiteheads, Mrs. Whitehead winked and said, "Give my best to King Kong!" Whitehead just laughed and said, "Forget the hairy ape. Keep your eyes wide for that Fay Wray. Now she's a *real* movie star." King Kong *would* be more fun than the wedding!

The flowers here are coming up faster than we can keep the weeds pulled. Your mother must be spending hours with hers again every night. Is she still putting giant bouquets of lilacs all through the house and baking her special meals for the week they bloom? My favorite part of the Whiteheads' garden is a long thick row of poppies as red as Christmas and always fluttering like butterflies. I can't wait to see them bloom this year.

Since my eyes are clouding up I'd better stop and get to bed.

> Be well and happy,
> My love as always,
> Bill

As he leisurely folded up the letter again, Willie remembered the thick odor of lilacs that had always filled the house in the spring. Until this summer Grom had always had some kind of flower in the house, but when her big lilac hedge bloomed she filled every vase she owned. She'd talk all year about that hedge like it was a talented child. The summer Grom started making Willie get his own switches for a spanking, he took them from the center of the hedge. He felt joy when he did it, but quickly said "no" when she asked him in tears about her damaged hedge.

Embarrassed by the memory, Willie stretched his back till it popped and tried to look bored. The next envelope held four postcards instead of a letter.

"New York!"

June 17, 1966

Dear Kate,

Well, this is it. Everything Ottawa and Berea are not. Since the wedding isn't until tomorrow, I went walking all over today till my knees gave out. The cement is

95

terrible. There are all kinds of people everywhere. I even saw men at one restaurant who were acting like couples. I found myself staring like the first time I saw Whitehead work on a chair. More later. . . . Bill

"No." Willie whined and tossed the card toward the door with a lifeless pitch. The friendship in the letters had kept Willie's fantasy family alive. It didn't even feel like they were divorced. So why, Willie wished, couldn't his father just keep to chairs. It was so much easier to think of him as his father when he didn't talk about men.

June 19, 1966

Dear Kate,
Since I couldn't find a post office to get any stamps and since the wedding is now over, you get three more cards and an envelope from the hotel. The wedding was as high and fancy as ours was plain. After the twentieth time of having to explain what I did for a living and that I wasn't married, I retreated to the kitchen. My cousin Liz was hiding too.

(third card)

After she went on and on about her black boyfriend, I decided to tell her about me. So much for that. I doubt if anyone's ever spit wedding cake so far across a room before!
The cute couple seemed to like their chair. They're going to make me an uncle in six months. Seems Mr. Perfect finally made a mistake. But since it's the first

grandchild, no one seems to care. They've already asked me to make it a child's rocking chair.

"Damn her!" Willie said in anger. *He* was the first grandchild.

"D—" he started to say again, but stopped. He wasn't sure if the "her" was Grom for telling him nothing, or his mother for saying he didn't exist. Willie yanked his chair forward and leaned his arms full against the table.

(fourth card)

If you ever get a chance to see New York, do it. It's been a good visit. My parents pushed for me to join them on their Nova Scotia vacation, but I'm eager to take the bus back home. A week of their questions is no vacation—especially when they don't want the truth.

> 'Bye for now.
> Bill

October 5, 1966

Dear Kate,
Congratulations on your promotion! I always knew you'd get your own desk someday. . . .

Willie sat up straight. "If I had *her* brains I could have passed trigonometry!"

I've meant to answer your last letters several times, but everything here has been inside out since I returned from New York. Mrs. Whitehead had a stroke while I was gone. She's back home now, and Whitehead hasn't left her side for more than a waking hour since it happened. His part of the shop seems stuck in time. He wouldn't even answer questions about orders and supplies till yesterday. It's as if her stroke stole away his interest in anything but her, like it stole away her speech. It's been hard to look at her, looking half dead and droopy, but the doctor says she's got a good chance of moving a bit and talking some again. She's already a little better, though depressed at needing so much help. We moved all her favorite things and her bed into the living room, where she can see her gardens from the window. . . .

Though his skin shone with a filmy sweat, Willie drew in his shoulders as if he were chilled. It hadn't even crossed his mind to move Grom's bed to the dining room with all the windows.

Whitehead works with her like he does with wood, knowing when to listen and when to push or support. He even gave in and got glasses for his "tired" eyes so he could read her the paper every night. Every now and then he'll make up some wild story to try and get her laughing. Last night he started reading her a made-up story about a new strip joint that was coming to town. When he told her she should audition, she got to laughing so hard and acting surprised that she moved more than she had in days. After that she slept the whole night through. The best news is that she can almost begin to make a fist again.

We both miss her cooking, but I do the best I can. I've even learned to fix grits, though I still can't bear to eat them. They both love them and it's something she can easily eat.

I'm hoping that even though you didn't mention Keith in your last letter, things are still working out between you two. There may be someone new in my life. I don't know how to explain it, but there's some kind of strong but good uneasiness between myself and the new druggist in town. He's started bringing Mrs. Whitehead's prescriptions out to the house after work every few days and staying to visit. The visits are good and relaxing. It's the good-byes that get tense, as if there is more going on than we're sure enough to say. . . .

Willie glanced toward Grom's room, which still flickered with the TV's light. It felt as if the letter had just described every day of their summer.

But enough of that. Best of wishes till next time.

Love,
Bill

P.S. I didn't mean to skip your birthday. It's just that the summer disappeared before I got to see it.

Thirsty again, Willie reached toward the refrigerator for another Coke. There were two left, but he pushed the door closed. A plain glass of water would taste better. He'd had enough bubbles and sweet caramel to last for days.

December 11, 1966

Dear Kate,
Happy holidays to you. The snow here is beautiful and unusual this early. There's even been time to enjoy

it since my mother convinced a shop in Philadelphia to sell some of our chairs, and for a lot more than we get around here.

We're going to have a typical quiet Whitehead Christmas here. Just the three of us and David Shoaltner. Mrs. Whitehead is better each week, though it's doubtful she'll ever be strong enough to walk again. Still, her spirits are good and Whitehead is beginning to work a little in the shop each day.

I'm sure things will be smoothed out between you and Keith by the time you read this letter. Seeing how hard your mom can be on you sometimes and how jealous she has become of your time, he may never like her that much. But that's because he *does* love you. He can probably tell she's just causing trouble to keep you at home. She can't expect you to stay with her forever just because your father didn't.

I don't know what to think about Evan—the druggist. He's become the best friend I have here. But if I tell him I love him, he could leave me or worse. Sometimes as we keep extending our good-bye conversations, his eyes look like he's afraid he's about to fall into a canyon. Who knows? Thanks for being there to listen. Best of wishes and holiday celebrations.

With love,
Bill

"Grom *is* jealous," said Willie. He thought back to the letters of his mother's visit to Berea. And then to Grom's yearly refusals to let him go to summer swim camp.

"Or afraid of being alone . . . of being left again."
Letter by letter the stiff-backed Grom who'd al-

ways been there—silent and sure—was wilting before his memories' eyes. She hadn't wanted his mother to grow up and go away any more than she'd wanted him to change or go away to college.

"No wonder she kept everything as still and the same as an old photograph." She wanted her world to always be there and the same, just like the picture of his mother and himself in the rocker was always there for Willie.

March 5, 1967

This letter came so long after the last one in December, Willie worried about its news. And, though he wanted the reading over with, the shrinking size of the letter stack made him feel uneasy.

Dear Kate,
This looks to be a historical spring for its quantity of good news. Have you and Keith chosen a date yet? If you wait till autumn, both the weather and your mother might have cooled down a bit. She's probably still afraid to live alone. But you know she'll be okay. She's stronger than she thinks she is.

As Whitehead would say, things are really "cracklin' " around here. Mrs. Whitehead is doing better than the doctor ever expected. She's been rubbing so much on those wooden shells I carved for her, her hands are getting as limber as the carvings are shiny. It was so fresh and sunny last Saturday that Whitehead took her on a picnic out under their favorite old tree. When they were late coming back, I went out to see if things were okay and found them curled up asleep in the shade. . . .

Willie stopped reading and slowly rolled his neck in a circle. He liked Mrs. Whitehead *and* the idea of them having a secret date. But as he lingered on the image of them curled together beneath the tree, he found himself growing frightened. It *seemed* so good, but sooner or later one would die and leave the other alone.

"Read!" he told himself aloud.

As for me, last week a Representative from Pennsylvania saw my chairs in the Philadelphia shop and commissioned me to make four matching chairs for his new home in Washington, D.C. I've got some walnut with a beautiful grain that's been waiting for the right project. It feels so good to be able to support myself now doing what I've dreamed of doing. And who knows what famous people might end up sitting in one of my chairs now!

I saw Larry last week when I was in town. I thought he'd already moved. He's changed his major *again* and won't graduate till May. He kept talking about two women he was dating and how he might marry one of them and go to grad school in Lexington. If he told me once, he told me ten times how happy he was, but he still wouldn't look me in the eyes when he talked. The good thing was that I didn't really care. It almost felt like I was talking to a stranger.

I decided I wanted the trouble with my family that's sure to come to get started. Then maybe it can end. As long as I kept myself a secret so they'd feel comfortable, *I* felt like a lie, so I figured they could be uncomfortable for a while. I wrote them over a month ago, but they haven't mentioned it in either of their letters. It's like my dad telling us that if we just stood still and ignored the bees, they'd go away and not sting us.

Enough of that stuff. I'll close for now with more cheers for your news. Promise to let me know as soon as you set your wedding date.

Love as
always,
Bill

May 13, 1967

Dear Kate,

I thought you'd want to know and I wanted to let you know that Mrs. Whitehead's gone. She had a massive stroke during the night last weekend and died on the way to the hospital. . . .

"But . . . " Willie tried to speak, but his breath gave way. Though she'd been gone for sixteen years, Willie felt like he'd just found her dead. His head throbbed with the same instant headache he'd had the morning he'd found Grom. "He'll never get to hold her again."

Whitehead just sat stone still, and when I went up to him he started cursing her for dying and refused to identify the body. I've never seen anyone hurt so bad. The next day he just walked around the farm without saying or eating anything. Then that night he walked in for supper like always and told me we had to get busy. We worked two full days nonstop to make her coffin, and all the time we worked he told me stories about her. They met at a picnic when he asked her to dance and she broke his toe. She felt so bad, she brought him a pie every day for a week. At the end of the week he asked her to break another toe so she'd keep coming to visit. They got married a month later. . . .

Willie couldn't remember Grom ever telling a story about his grandfather. It was only through Libby that he'd even learned of how he and Grom eloped. When Grom *had* referred to him, her eyes had always been cold, never polished the way his dad had said Shoaltner's were. Even though his grandfather could still be alive—somewhere—Grom had told no stories to make him *seem* dead, as she had with his dad. The only one she'd kept alive with stories was Willie's mother, who was the only one who had really died.

When we were done, he marked the remaining oak planks and told me as firm as he'd ever said anything that the rest of the wood was for me to make his when his time came so they could be buried in one tree together. . . .

Willie caught himself shuffling his feet on the clammy floor.

"I need a swim," he told himself. Still, he stayed at the table. He tried to read on, but he couldn't stop thinking of Whitehead alone. Of Grom alone if he'd gone to college before she'd died. Of his father alone though surrounded by people. Of himself alone now.

"Just read!"

Three times as many people came to her funeral as were ever at one of her big Thanksgiving dinners. Before anyone had arrived, and when he thought he was alone, Whitehead put a little box in her coffin, saying "Goodbye, love. I couldn't have asked for a life any better than the love we shared." When he turned around and saw me, I was embarrassed, but he just smiled and said, "I couldn't let her leave without her seashells and that scarf with the butterflies she loved so much." I'm not sure when or how things will ever feel normal around here again. I miss her so much and miss taking care of her. Take care.

Yours as ever,
Bill

P.S. Whitehead told me I should take the carved shells I'd made for her. One will be coming in the mail to you.

Willie searched his memory for a wooden seashell. In the dresser? The desk? Tripping over the heap of boxes in the hall, Willie hurried upstairs. Back in his mother's gutted room he quickly but carefully emptied each box onto the bed. Rummaged its contents. Put it all back and then emptied the next. Nothing.

"The letter box!" Willie ran back down the stairs two and three at a time.

"Who knows how small it might be."

But it wasn't in the box. Maybe she'd given it to him along with the rocker? Had *he* lost it as he had so many toys?

Willie grabbed the next envelope.

"It's just a fake shell," he told himself. "Forget it!"

He was more angry at himself for being upset— for wanting it—than he was at not finding the shell. If only he were already swimming laps.

Willie groaned when he saw the envelope's birthday card. It was covered with candles and party balloons.

July 2, 1967

Dear Kate,

Happy Birthday to you! You may be another year older, but remember you're still five months younger than me.

As ever,
Bill

As he put the card down, Willie noticed the writing that covered the back.

P.S. Thanks for your card to Whitehead. He was pleased that you remembered her so kindly. Me too. And thanks for asking about Evan. I tried to talk about how some people are different and how some men can be special friends, but he didn't respond. Still, he keeps coming by even when there's no prescription to bring, and things still feel (for me) the same between us. I love sharing time with him, and thinking of him always makes me smile. I'm even having dreams about him. I want him to come visit, but I also wish he wouldn't with everything feeling so confused.

July 12, 1967

Dear Kate,

The shop in town is selling these cards of old quilts now, and I thought you'd like one. The summer keeps chugging along with chairs and gardening. Why we planted so much, I'll never know. We've got enough okra to gag a horse. Last week brought a bonus, though. When I took a basket of tomatoes over to Shoaltner, the time felt right to talk with him. He just listened as I stumbled over words, then said, "Someday the right man will come and you'll know *and* know it was worth the wait. Quiet is the only way." His voice felt like a wall crumbling down. When I told him about Evan and how I couldn't tell what was what, he gave me a kiss and hugged me tight. It felt like I was finally home. My love to you with cheers,

Bill

Willie sat staring at the walls he'd always called home. Filled with nothing but silence and night, the house seemed as hollow as an empty pool. Every sound echoed. Willie listened to himself breathe a slow sigh and tried to think of nothing but the city pool. Cool and still. The same as he'd always known it.

Willie had now grown so used to the story in the letters excluding him, he made no connection with the date being so near his second birthday.

Dear Kate,

It feels like someone has flung open all the windows and a strong breeze is blowing in. I finally told Evan that I loved him and hoped he had feelings for me. I must have sweated fifty buckets in thirty seconds. Then he said, "Yes." I can't believe it. We talked and talked and talked for hours. He'd been as nervous as I've been and has never known any other men like us. It was such a wonderful night. . . .

"Damn queers," muttered Willie. They were the last thing he wanted to think about now. The dates of the letters were getting closer and closer to the date on his mother's gravestone. Still, as soon as he'd said "Damn queers," he wished he hadn't and was glad no one had heard him. Meaning to or not, Willie had lived too much of his father's life through the letters to dismiss him like that.

It was—it is—just like you said about Keith. Being with him feels so bright and alive, so safe and warm that . . .

As he read, Willie's mind and body filled with memories of being with Libby. Those times had felt like gliding through water. So safe that nothing else had mattered. *Then* he'd been sure he'd never be left again. He was angry at Libby for ending those times; then, remembering he was the one who had left her, he cursed himself.

"Damn it. Why'd you have to leave? Why'd you have to kill it?"

Willie sadly returned to the letter. He had no answer.

. . . so safe and warm that making love *is* the truest thing to do no matter what anybody else says.

When I got back home the next morning, Whitehead was all upset, worrying about where I'd been. Everything felt so right, I told him. He just kept eating. And I immediately wished I'd kept my big mouth shut. When I tried to explain things, he said, "I was just worried you were hurt. Don't figure the rest has anything to do with me as long as you do your work." But it does. It's me.

All in all Whitehead is doing well. He's taken to just working when it's cool in the morning and doing whatever he fancies the rest of the day. He seems happy, though he's still sleeping in his chair downstairs instead of their empty bed. Mainly he's been planning a big flower garden for spring. He wants a dozen of every kind Mrs. Whitehead loved. Come spring . . .

Willie saw Grom's yard clearly in his mind, but it wasn't complete. The garden would never be the same again even if the flowers remained the same. The garden was the flowers *and* Grom with her knees in the dirt and her yellow sun hat shining like the biggest bloom.

Come spring this place will look like a nursery. Keep enjoying your trips to the reservoir. You'll soon look like walnut carvings!

Smiles and love,
Bill

August 25, 1967

Dear Kate,

I'm glad to hear that your mother is easing up. Surely once you're married she'll let herself believe that you really love one another. Will you try to find a house or live in the apartment over Keith's barbershop? . . .

"The barbershop!" said Willie, suddenly remembering the thick mixture of smells he'd loved. "The 'white man' [as he'd called him because of his barber's coat] would have been my step . . . father."

Things are steady here. Always another chair to make. . . .

Willie tried to read the words again, but he couldn't stop thinking about the barbershop.

"And the spin-me chair!" he said with a laugh. How, he wondered, could he have forgotten that? He could hear his mother and the "white man" laughing warmly as he bounced in the giant barber's chair. He'd loved it all. Especially all the mirrors and the jar of Tootsie Rolls.

"The Tootsie Rolls!" The memories were thick and so fresh. He kept saying it as he nodded, smiling.

But choked on his words when he noticed the shoe box was empty. At that moment he'd have traded anything to fill it up again. Anything. The end of the letters meant his mother's death and still no certain answers.

If only he could have rewritten the letters, he told himself, and made a better ending. If only there were more letters to be found. But he knew as he stared at the empty box that there was nothing he could have done, or do, to change the past. There was nothing he could do to bring his mother back beyond his father's words.

"Things are steady here," he read aloud. He had to hear a voice, even if it was only his own.

"Things are steady here," he read again, lowering his voice to keep control.

Always another chair to make. The set for the Representative is almost done, but my favorite project is a rocker I've almost finished for Shoaltner. Last month when we were talking, he gave me a candle holder that his "brother" George had carved for him on their twenty-fifth anniversary. My rocker will be his surprise present in return. I've tried to make the arms a bit wider to fit his old callused hands and the seat a bit higher from the floor to help him get in and out. Evan says Shoaltner's arthritis is getting worse, though Shoaltner would never say a word.

Things are good with Evan. Thanks for asking. We get to see each other almost every day for supper. Sometimes for breakfast, and Whitehead doesn't seem to mind him here. At least he never says he does. I'm just hoping that Evan doesn't get the job in Louisville he applied for several months ago. I can't leave the shop and Whitehead. But there's not much to do but wait and let time tell.

I hope all your wedding plans are going smoothly. Are you still planning a honeymoon trip to St. Louis?

Take care. And don't worry about your mother being alone. No matter where you live in Ottawa, it won't be very far from her.

Yours as ever,
Bill

"As ever . . ." echoed Willie.

He had been preparing himself for some grand conclusion, but the letters had simply stopped when she was no longer there to answer them. Stopped as still as the night. A silence still loud with questions.

Willie's hands went numb as he slowly refolded the final letter. So much, he thought, in so few pages. One by one he returned each letter to the old shoe box—each seeming twice as heavy as before he'd read it. Then, after a long final look, he returned the picture of his father and Larry. And gently closed the lid.

"No need to keep it," Willie told himself as he looked at his father's image—his own—reflected in the window. "No need."

6

Willie had always climbed the pool fence easily, but this time he wobbled as he stepped over the top. He was thinking of all the nights he'd gone cross-town and climbed this fence after telling Grom he was going out with friends. As he jumped down, his gym shorts caught on the fence and ripped straight to the waist.

"Damn!" he yelled as he landed off-balance, scraping both knees. He hated making simple mistakes.

Willie sucked in his breath and stared into the water. As he looked straight down, it was almost invisible with no way to tell its depth. It was exactly the clear, calm wetness he'd looked forward to since his shower last night. The escape he'd wanted more and more with each letter he'd read. If only his thoughts could be as clear. One moment he was convinced that he only *thought* he'd read of such people and things in the letters. The next moment they all screamed for his attention. He'd wanted answers and had gotten them, but each answer had only divided itself into more questions. Nothing he'd known before as fact was true anymore.

As he sat down in the darkness that framed the pool's light, he told himself "No." He couldn't cry.

"You're just tired."

He'd gone this long without knowing anything about his parents. What difference did it make now? They'd all lied anyway. Grom about his father. His mother about himself. His father about—

"Forget it," he told himself, and wedged off his shoes.

Quickly he pulled off his T-shirt and dove into the pool with barely a splash. Water. It felt so good to be light again. To be moving and slick. Willie skimmed the pool's surface thinking only of the rhythm—arm over arm and the alternating sounds of air sucked in in silence, then blown back out as bubbles roared.

When he reached the pool's far side, Willie turned and pushed off but left his legs limp. His numbness had turned to anger again. Arm over arm he fought his way through the water, feeling more in command with the force of each stroke.

Willie's single largest memory was of feeling shut

out. It was as if he'd grown up forced to sit outside in the hall while his family was inside talking. No matter what he'd been told, he'd known there was always more going on that Grom was keeping from him. And now, though the letters had pulled him inside from that hall, he wasn't really a part of his family after all. No one had made a place for him. He still had no story that felt like home.

The box of letters had changed Grom like ice to water and back again. Had told him of people in love and confused. But it was all just scraps. An ugly jumble that would make people wag their heads if they knew.

Willie wished now that there hadn't been any letters to find. What was he supposed to do with a father who didn't even know he's a father? A father who was gay? A name and a face still weren't a father anyway. There was still no voice to scold or comfort. No one there for him to help, or to help him.

Though his arms were growing heavy and his shoulders burned, Willie kept swimming lap after lap. As he tired, he began to imagine rocking in his chair when he got back home. Thinking of that always helped to keep his rhythm sure, but this time he saw his father as well.

His father was sanding the rocker over and over and over again. Then writing a letter and sanding again. Willie tried to erase him—to see only the chair—but as he watched his father fade away, Willie realized that *he* had taken his place by the chair. Now Willie was sanding. Then his father again. People and voices kept crowding close. Now Grom began yelling, "Throw it out. Throw it out!" But his mother was in it, in the short blue dress. Then his father. No matter how he tried, Willie couldn't get close to the chair. Couldn't reach it. Reach *them.* They couldn't *see* him. Still, all the time his father kept sanding. Louder and louder. Then Grom began yelling, "Throw it out!" again. Willie screamed, "Let me in!" Then BANG. A door slammed shut right in front of his face.

Startled, Willie broke his rhythm, sucked in water and began to choke as his thoughts whirled around.

"Damn them. Forget them!" he yelled as he coughed, slapping his fist against the water again and again.

When he could finally draw a deep breath again, Willie held it in and let himself sink. Below, everything was quiet and still. His world alone. Slowly he rolled over and looked up toward the night. From beneath the surface, the top of the water looked heavy and thick like a silvery cover that could seal him inside.

Willie pushed off the bottom, broke through the surface and gulped in air. In two more strokes he'd reached the edge and pulled himself out. From above, the water's surface still looked as thin as light. *If* he stared straight down. But when he glanced to the right or left, the water looked gray, too rippled and too thick to see through.

Within moments he was feeling very tired.

"Too much work."

Willie wadded his shirt into a pillow and lay down along the pool's edge. Watching the water change color and shape, he began to remember the first time Grom had dragged him to that same pool.

That day the water had looked almost as blue as his crayon. He'd refused to get into the water at all.

"We're in the shallow end," Grom explained. "The water won't even come up to your shoulders."

"I don't want to turn blue."

"Who would?" She retied her sun hat. "Now, get in the water so you can learn to float. You can use the ladder."

"But the *water's* blue. I don't want to get blue."

Grom rolled her eyes. "Why would you? No one else in the pool has turned blue."

"For true?"

"For true," she told him. "Now are you ready?"

She reasoned for nearly half an hour while Willie stared at the water and shook his head. Tired of it all, Grom finally dumped her tea on the ground. Then, by magic as far as Willie was able to figure out then, she showed him that glass by glass the blue water of the pool was just as clear as the water she sprayed from the hose at home.

"For true?"

"For true. Did my hand turn blue?"

"No."

Even so it was two more visits to the pool before he stopped worrying about turning blue or sinking, and learned to relax enough to float.

Grom had taken him every day that summer, always watching and waving to prove he was safe. Willie felt his whole face smiling at the memory. She'd been so proud the day he'd swum out and rescued her soggy sun hat that she'd made him a cake with icing like waves.

As his thoughts returned to the present, he noticed how the light from the pool lamps sent thin discs of color everywhere, shimmering like schools of transparent fish. At the same time, far below that, he could see wiggling shadows. The proof of currents that couldn't be seen. As he dipped in his hand, the smallest of gestures changed everything, sending thin waves of silver to the other side.

Each time, each way he looked at the water, its color changed as quickly as the truths in the letters had changed. Again Willie thought of all the blue water that had turned clear in Grom's tea glass. The water was none of the colors *and* all of them. He'd seen them, seen them change.

"Maybe none of the letters are true?"

Willie lay back down and stared at the sky.

"*Or* all of them . . . sometimes . . . in some way."
It had to be true that his father was alive.

Willie sighed with pleasure as he let the poolside cement support his back and heavy head. He wanted to empty his mind, make it as clear as the water in Grom's tea glass, but all he'd read in the letters kept sliding in and out. Kept muddying all he'd known before.

"Who cares . . ." Willie whispered as he quickly began to knead himself.

As the poster of the woman in the red swimsuit came to mind, all wet and alive, Willie smiled and arched his back. This was good. Everything was fading but the swelling in his hand. Then just as quickly he saw the poster torn up in the trash. Saw the train-covered wall. Saw the shell that had been his life-long room. Saw Libby. He tried to imagine the poster again, to stroke himself back to hardness, but it was no use. Now even that had left him.

As he lazily pulled on his shoes, Willie thought of the door to his mother's room.

"All those years."

He'd passed it thousands of times while the letters were waiting inside to be read. To have always been so near and so far from knowing about his father. About his mother. From really knowing Grom.

The more he tried to sort through the night of letters, the more it seemed to Willie like a giant joke of good news and bad. It was bad Grom had been so secretive and bad that she'd kept the room locked. But it was also good that she'd locked it up like a tomb and saved the letters by accident. If she hadn't, she would have cleaned it, found the letters and thrown them out. Then Willie never would have found them or read them.

Was it good news or bad news that his mother had kept them at all? Why would she have kept the letters if she was marrying somebody else? Had she kept them for *him*? Willie laughed.

"Happy Birthday, Willie!" he jeered. "Your father's not dead after all—just gay. Here's the proof."

But Willie knew his mother wouldn't have told him his father was dead. She'd given him his father's rocker and name. He knew from the letters—that she'd written to him and kept his—that she wasn't ashamed of his father. Yes. He felt certain his mother would have told him the truth. At least bit by bit. After all, she told Keith.

The realization of how close he'd come to *not* finding the letters in his hurry to pack up the house and leave left Willie embarrassed. He could have accidentally kept Grom's life of lies alive. If he *hadn't* seen them, he told himself, and had tossed the box of letters in a pile for the sale, a stranger could have read them. Even worse, *they'd* have seen only the surface. No one else would have known how the letters brought his father back from the dead. Or how the last one marked his mother's death. No one else would have had *his* life to give the letters meaning.

As the sky became more day than night, the water in the pool changed its colors again.

"Come on," he told himself as he tied his T-shirt around his torn shorts. "It's almost over."

Then he climbed up the fence and dropped to the grass.

By the time Willie was halfway home, the sun was burning whiter and hotter than it had the day before. The only cool spot he could see was his own thin shadow that stretched ahead for half the block. At least, he consoled himself, he wouldn't be roofing. His arms and legs were already feeling too thick for much work.

"A shower ... a cold-coffee shower." Willie chuckled to himself. He had to find something to wake him up or he'd bleed to death shaving.

A glimpse of his reflection in a store window sent Willie's thoughts to Kentucky. Somewhere—Berea—his father must be waking up. Next to Evan? Thinking of coffee and needing to shave like Willie. Trying to get his day going too.

"Unless," said Willie to his reflection, "he still has his beard."

In the early sun the house shone as white as a

blank movie screen and made Grom's lilac hedge look twice as green. All the flowers looked fresh again after hours in the darkness. There was even the first chrysanthemum bud pushing out some gold.

"Willie?" called Paul from the side of the yard. "Willie. You look like hell."

"Sorry I'm late. Did Libby call?"

"Is she helping too?"

"No . . . I just wondered." Surely she'd show up by noon.

Paul looked again at Willie's scraped knees and ragged face.

"Were you in a fight?"

"No. Just up all night packing her crap."

"Well, it *looks* like a fight."

When they reached the front door, Willie hurriedly joked, "I kind of got in a hurry."

In the daylight the crooked pile of dropped boxes looked more like a trash heap than someone's carefully guarded past.

"You mean all this is your grandmother's stuff? There's enough here for two sales."

The first box Paul tried to pick up broke open, spilling years of *TV Guide* magazines.

"Is there anything she didn't keep?"

Willie barely heard him. When he'd first seen Paul in the yard, Willie's thoughts had skipped for a moment and erased the whole night of letters. For a moment everything was again as he'd known it to be and he felt in charge. But as he came back into the house, Willie sensed a swelling of sound, as if everyone were calling out to him.

"Let's go get some breakfast."

"Don't need to," explained Paul. "My mom had another one of her Betty Crocker attacks. She sent over muffins, fruit and sausages. *And* eggs if we hurry up and eat them before they turn to rubber."

"But I need to go . . . and get some coffee."

"*And* coffee," said Paul as he opened the basket. "Sit down."

Willie ate quickly without tasting much, while Paul chatted on about his parents' most recent argument. Everywhere Willie looked, the house looked like an old frame with its picture gone. What remained was stacked and piled and falling all over. Except for his rocking chair. He'd left it sitting empty.

"The rocking chair in the living room *stays*," he told Paul.

Willie left the kitchen to go see it again.

"Along with my clothes and stereo."

"Sure. More coffee?"

Again Willie didn't hear him. His rocking chair seemed both so old *and* so new. Older than Willie, but new to his eyes. It hadn't worn out, but now he saw how much had worn in. The shine of his rubbing hands and head. The scuff of his shoes. He moved nearer to touch it.

123

"More coffee?" Paul called again from the kitchen.

"Yeah. Sure. Then we'd better get started."

He was glad Paul was there and just as glad they'd never talked very much. Now that Willie knew about his parents and didn't have to invent his past, he didn't know what to tell.

"Thanks for being here—"

"Sure."

"I mean to help. Ready?"

"Ready."

Each headed outside with a big box, but Willie slowed down as he passed Grom's patch of blue flowers. He was filled with thoughts of the pool again. He could no more figure out what color to make the water if he had to paint a picture to show real water than he could figure out what was true about his parents or what to say about them. The only thing Willie felt certain wouldn't change now was the fact that he'd read the letters. Nothing that could happen could erase the past night.

Willie set the box down at the far edge of the yard, then hurried inside. He was putting the shoe box of letters beneath his rocking chair when he heard Paul walk in, then begin to laugh.

"Paul," said Willie, "let's do the big furniture first. Get the heavy stuff done, then the rest will seem easy."

Paul was still laughing.

"What's so funny?"

"If you keep flashing your ass like that, the neighbors'll think you're a lunar eclipse!"

"Damn," muttered Willie, grabbing for some jeans in his box of clothes. He'd forgotten about snagging his shorts at the pool. "Always what'll the neighbors think."

Willie sat rocking. The house felt completely quiet now except for the auctioneer's chant of the past being sold.

People had been milling around and picking at things since Willie and Paul had carried the first piece of furniture out to the yard.

"SOLD!" Each time the word rang out like a hammered nail.

Under the bright sun and the stares of strangers the furniture looked so limp and forlorn. Willie had watched the sale for a while, but it was cooler inside. More, he didn't want to know who bought what. He wanted to leave everything, not drive by some house and know that Grom's sofa or bed was inside—being used by a stranger.

At the sound of the door Willie looked up. It

was another person coming to see what was left in the house. Willie stared straight at him.

"Everything for sale is already outside."

The people were as bad as termites, all eager to swallow up the house. They didn't even watch where they were walking in the yard. The third time he found somebody standing *in* one of Grom's flower beds, Willie had brought the boxes of vases back into the house. Then he'd picked every flower. Now fourteen vases each filled with a single color were sitting around the living room.

Willie was looking at the flowers and wishing for a storm to come blow the crowd away when he heard the door again.

"Everything for sale is already *outside!*"

"Willie?"

It was Libby!

"Willie. It's me," she said as she came into the living room with a thermos and cups.

She looked wonderful. He wanted to jump up and hold her and be held, but he couldn't leave his rocker. He wanted to talk, but the words wouldn't come.

"You've got more flowers here than they had at the prom." Libby walked closer and laughed. "You want to do the Toilet Paper Tango again?"

Willie's eyes kept darting between the flowers and her feet.

"How's the sale going?"

"Fast."

He couldn't let their eyes meet, couldn't dare to have her see into him. He was embarrassed and afraid to see her look of caring.

"How are you?" she asked as she leaned forward and kissed his head. "Besides tired?"

Every gesture she made, every sound, made Willie feel more vulnerable. He knew that if he let his mind drift for a second, he'd start to cry.

"It's . . ." Willie tried to talk, but the only choice was silence or tears.

He just kept rocking and listening to the chant of the auctioneer.

"SOLD!"

Willie jumped. Neither he nor Libby knew what to say next.

Finally, Libby sat down on the floor near Willie. "This is a great rocker."

"My dad didn't die," blurted Willie. Just the mention of the chair had sucked the words from his mouth.

"But you told me—"

"He wrote letters to my mother for two years after I was born. Till just before she died."

Libby scooted closer.

"You mean your grandmother lied?"

The question seemed so simple.

"Like a thief," whispered Willie, embarrassed by his answer's truth.

"But if your dad was alive, then why didn't he take care of you?"

"He didn't know—doesn't know—I was born."

Libby watched his eyes. They were racing miles away.

"My mom never told him," Willie continued. "She was pregnant when they got divorced."

"But why not? Was he awful?"

"No . . . no." As always when they talked, Libby's short direct questions brought equally compact answers. They were the same questions he'd been asking himself, but Libby's voice made the answers somehow easier to hear.

"She loved him." Willie let the words echo in his ears.

"But why didn't your grandmother want you to know your dad was alive?"

"She . . ." Willie stopped rocking and looked again at the vase of blue flowers. "She was protecting me."

Like the blue pool water that seemed to suddenly turn clear when put in a glass, when he compared the woman he'd known to what the letters revealed, Willie now saw Grom anew. No matter what color the water looked like, it always came back to the same clear glass.

"She loved me."

"More than anything else in the world," said Libby. She slowly opened the thermos and poured them both some tea. "But what was she protecting you from?"

Another shout of "SOLD!" rang through the house.

"It doesn't matter anymore," said Willie, beginning to rock again.

"Well, did the letters say why your mom never told your dad you were born?"

Willie knew from the letters there had to be many reasons, but again the shortest was also the truest, the clearest.

"She loved him. She gave me his name and chair."

Willie's face brightened up for a moment, then froze again. They both knew the next question.

"Are you going to tell him? Go see him?"

"We have the same face" was all he could say. "He makes chairs in Kentucky. Even for congressmen. He made this chair."

By instinct he was caressing the chair's warm wooden arms.

"I guess *that's* why Grom would never sit in it. Even when I was sick that time three years ago and she stayed by my bed all day and all night. She dragged another chair all the way upstairs instead of sitting in my—in his rocker."

"Are you going to see him?"

"He's the only one who can tell me about my mother."

Willie felt like he was standing on the edge of the highest high dive. Everything felt so far away—

so uncertain. Every shout of "SOLD!" made Grom—made home—feel farther away.

"Grom was the one who made me learn how to swim." He *had* to talk of her—had to make her feel near.

"When I was little, she'd come to every swim meet. Once . . ." Willie laughed and, forgetting, almost looked into Libby's eyes. "Once she got so excited when I finally won third place, she ran down to meet me at the pool. If the coach hadn't grabbed her, she'd have done a half gainer in the shallow end."

Slowly Willie was beginning to relax. Word by word his voice felt more like his own again.

"Even in high school on the days of a meet she'd always cook the holiday breakfast she made when her lilacs bloomed. Bacon and eggs. Giant biscuits with apricot jam. And an apple baked full of cinnamon and raisins. Gold ones. She always got the gold ones."

Then, just as quickly as his words had come, they stopped. Willie hated the silence. He wished Libby would just go ahead and ask the next question. Get it over with. Everything seemed to come down to the same "why." Why did they get divorced? Why did Grom say he was dead?

But what would Libby think, he worried, or say if he told her the truth? She could laugh. She could leave him. Like he'd told her before, it didn't matter. But still it did.

"He loved my mom," he said softly, "but he was . . . gay."

Willie breathed deeply. He'd said it aloud to another person. For a heavy moment both were quiet; then Libby spoke as plainly as she always did.

"That's hard. But it's not reason enough to pretend that somebody's dead. What was your grandmother afraid he'd do?"

"I don't know. She did the same thing about my grandfather," said Willie, offering a defense. "When *he* left her to marry somebody else."

"Like your dad left you to be with somebody else?"

"But he didn't know he was leaving me. My mom never told him. And she never told . . . " Willie stopped. He wasn't the only one who hadn't been told the truth. Maybe the answer to "why" wasn't always the same, or only one answer. "Grom. I bet she never told Grom she'd lied to him about me . . . so Grom would leave my dad alone. Grom never knew that *he* never knew. She only thought he left me."

Willie grinned. Once again the truth had changed like in Larry's old joke of good news and bad.

"So she just pretended they were dead? Cut them off and erased their lives?"

"She did it," said Willie, remembering, now, the

night he'd called Libby to break it off. "She had to end it so it didn't feel like they were always leaving her. She erased everything about anyone who left her. She kept that whole yard of stuff out there, but nothing about my grandfather. Nothing about my father. Nothing about my mother except her room. No photographs. Nothing personal from before my mother died except for my rocking chair, which I *made* her keep, a few old vases like the one she gave you, and her old cigar box of . . . my *grandfather's* old cigar box of her crochet things!"

Willie was up and walking out the door.

"I've got to find out if it's already been sold."

Unsure of where to look or even what she'd be looking for, Libby stayed put and listened for his voice. Within minutes he was back and beaming, holding a trowel and an old cigar box.

"You found it?"

"The neighbor lady had bought it in the box of doilies. I traded her the buffet she was still waiting to buy. Can you wait? I have to go to the cemetery. Will you wait?"

Willie was talking as fast as the auctioneer. He reached beneath his rocker and grabbed the shoe box like a lost treasure found. Then he stopped, looked straight into Libby's eyes and kissed her.

"I'll be back. Here. Sit in the rocker. Please. Will you wait?"

Libby smiled with a nod. Willie was out the door

and starting his car before she noticed that he hadn't taken even one vase of flowers.

Libby called from the porch. Willie heard her, but didn't stop. He had all he needed.

Driving over the old cobblestone streets toward the south edge of town, Willie replayed his annual trips there with Grom. Memorial Day—the one time she'd go each year—they'd plant new cuttings from her favorite geraniums. Grom had always said she didn't have the time to go more often. Now he knew she'd paid her respects every month in a different way. Every time she'd cleaned his mother's room and locked the door again.

The past that Grom had kept secret and lifeless behind that door, and even more she'd not even known herself, was now his, whether Willie wanted it or not. As he'd read the letters, he'd lived their lives in all their changing colors. Their past was now his present. His to keep as need and memory sanded and shaped it to make the family story that would feel as comfortable to him as his rocking chair.

At the edge of town the sky opened out and fields of wheat replaced backyards. The cobblestone turned to the hush of new pavement, then to the popping gravel of the cemetery drive.

Willie stopped the car just inside the gate. One stone, two graves. One already sunken with time and the other still high with earth and its wilted blanket of funeral flowers. Never had he felt so painfully alone. Or so much a part of his family.

Alone in the quiet Willie stared at the graves and began to cry. This time with no thoughts of trying to stop. He cried in silence for his mother and Grom. Cried *with* them too for all they'd lost. Cried for his father and cried for himself.

He cried as slowly he began to smile, knelt on the ground, and began to dig holes for the shoe box of letters and cigar box of threads as dearly and deliberately as only one in love can do.

"For you . . ." he whispered as he covered the hole by each grave. "For you to keep."

Then, as if in trade, he snapped off a sprig of the geranium. He knew a clear glass of water would bring new blooms.